BRIDESMAID FOR HIRE

THE ALMOST WIVES CLUB, BOOK 3

NANCY WARREN

AMBLESIDE PUBLISHING

Bridesmaid for Hire, The Almost Wives Club Book 3

ISBN: ebook 978-1-928145-14-1

ISBN: print 978-1-928145-15-8

Cover Design by Kim Killion

Ambleside Publishing

FOREWORD

Every day, as the days roll on,

Bridesmaids' garb we gaily don,

Sure that a maid so fairly famed Can't long remain unclaimed.

— GILBERT & SULLIVAN, RUDDIGORE

CHAPTER 1

Jasmine Ford did not think of herself as a superstitious woman, but, as she stood in Ashley Carnarvon's bedroom, holding the runaway bride's hastily discarded wedding gown, it occurred to her that this was her thirteenth time being a bridesmaid. And this wedding hadn't turned out to be very lucky.

This was definitely the first time she'd been left holding an empty wedding dress while the bride fled out the window. Through the still-open window, she could hear the sound of an engine fading as the getaway car headed further away. She could also hear the determined strains of music from the chamber quartet playing on the grounds of the Carnarvon estate, where two hundred guests, another pair of brides-maids, matching groomsmen and, oh Lord, a groom, stood waiting for a bride who was not going to show up. Tasmine was conscious of a wild urge to dump the designer dress on the bed and escape out that window herself.

A light breeze blew in from the ocean that fronted the Carnarvon estate in Malibu, making the dress shiver in her arms like an abandoned lover. It was such a beautiful dress, too. The silk was exquisite, the lace hand sewn, and at least a hundred real pearls decorated the bodice. Tasmine had seen a lot of wedding dresses in her time, but none as stunning as this one. The dress even smelled like a perfect wedding. Ever-so-slightly floral with a hint of spice.

Tasmine pulled in a breath, so her ribs hit the bodice of her bridesmaid dress. She wouldn't have chosen the brides-maids' dresses herself, they were black and fitted in the bodice with a white chiffon skirt worn with black heels. She'd made sure each dress fit, that both of the other bridesmaids had the correct shoes, hose and undergarments and she'd personally delivered the dresses and made the other bridesmaids try them on in front of her so any mistakes could be remedied. It had all gone so smoothly she should have worried. Weddings weren't supposed to run so perfectly in the planning stage. There were always hitches, but not with this one.

Tasmine had started her business, Bridesmaid for Hire, on a whim after she'd ended up organizing yet another wedding when she'd been asked to be a bridesmaid. She saw firsthand that most bridesmaids were too busy, or too flakey, to be a real help to the bride. Even though she also had a full-time job, she was organized enough that she could take on a lot of the duties without breaking a sweat.

A friend of that bride had come up to her after the wedding and suggested that, even though they weren't friends, she'd like Tasmine to be her bridesmaid. "I thought a thousand dollars would be fair. What do you think?"

Tasmine thought earning a thousand bucks for something she enjoyed doing was a great idea. It was amazing how word spread and soon she was an in-demand bridesmaid. She sat down, wrote up a business plan, and came up with a set of service packages: everything from simply showing up on the special day to organizing parts or all of the wedding. She loved organizing and attending weddings and her side hustle was starting to make her a decent second income. She never advertised—she didn't have to. Her name was mysteriously passed along from bride to bride. Many of them had become personal friends in the process.

Ashley had been so easy going. Too easy going she now realized. Like she wasn't really invested in the ceremony, which recent events now proved she wasn't. Eric was handsome in black tie and tails and stayed out of the way. The two mothers had got on well and shared similar tastes.

The venue was the Carnarvon estate, and Millicent and Duncan Carnarvon were seasoned entertainers who knew exactly where the tents should go, and where the best spot was for the chamber orchestra. They'd hired a company who did all their events and everything had arrived on time, as ordered.

Even the damn weather was flawless. A perfect California day with not a cloud in the sky.

She should have known that so many good things in a row were a bad omen.

As much as she wanted to throw off her own fancy gown and escape out the window in Ashley's wake, she didn't. Tasmine was not the runaway type. Grace Van Hoffendam, the groom's mother, had hired her as part wedding consultant and part bridesmaid. Tasmine had taken up being a professional bridesmaid because she had such a flare for organization, and no matter what happened, she never panicked. However, she'd never been in a situation quite like this before and she could feel panic fluttering behind her ribcage like a trapped bird. She tried to organize her scattered wits.

First thing she had to do was to quit clutching this dress as though it were a silk and lace life preserver. She found a white satin hanger and carefully placed the gown on it. There was no time to tuck the acres of silk into the fancy bag with the *oh-so-desirable* logo, the simple name of the wedding designer, Evangeline, in elegant script. With great care, she hung the dress from the open door of the wardrobe. What she needed to do, and fast, was to alert Grace Van Hoffendam or somebody to the current catastrophe. No one would know better how to deal with this crisis with the minimum embarrassment. Not that there wasn't going to be a huge dose of embarrassment, mostly for the poor, jilted groom standing there fidgeting in his finery.

She took a hasty step towards the door of the cottage that Ashley and her mother had shared on the Carnarvon estate. She wanted to make sure that Eric got the bad news as soon as possible so that he could quietly slip away before all two hundred of the extremely socially, politically, and economically powerful guests at the wedding realized he'd been made a complete fool of.

Marshaling her wits, she planted a calm smile on her face, took a deep breath, and opened the front door. She squeaked in alarm when she nearly bashed into Eric Van Hoffendam coming into the cottage as she was going out.

She immediately flew into traditional bridesmaid role. "Eric! What are you doing here? Don't you know it's bad luck to see the bride before the wedding?"

She stared up at him and her heart sped up as it always did when he was around. She couldn't help herself, he was so gorgeous. Even though he wasn't usually the best-dressed guy around, Eric was still hot. But in a black tie, with freshly trimmed hair and his beard barbered down to smooth stubble, the man was absolutely gorgeous. His blue eyes were the color of the summer sky, his body tall and straight on this day of all days, the day that he would begin life as a married man.

Except, he wouldn't.

And she was the only one who knew that. How she wished she had remained with the other bridesmaids, and not rushed back to make sure everything was okay with the bride. When Ashley had claimed she wanted a couple of minutes to herself, when she'd urged her three bridesmaids to go ahead and she'd be right there, Tasmine had experienced a tiny buzz of alarm. That was all it had been, like a whisper so faint, she could barely hear it. But, with a dozen weddings under her belt, she had an instinct for trouble. Not that she'd expected anything more than that maybe Ashley was going to kiss her favorite teddy bear goodbye, or shed a few tears over leaving her home.

Never in her wildest dreams could she have pictured any woman, never mind Ashley, running away from a chance to be with Eric.

The groom sent her a lightning-quick grin, the kind that let him get away with murder. "Nobody needs to know I was here. I just want to make sure Ash is okay."

All right, so she wasn't the only one with a nose for trouble. She gazed up at him and could not find the words. She remained rooted, mute.

Perhaps he read something in her expression, for his sunny blue eyes clouded and he gently but firmly moved her out of his way and walked into Ashley's bedroom.

She didn't know what to do but follow him.

When she got to the doorway, she paused. He stood in the center of Ashley's room turning in a slow circle, obviously noting that his bride wasn't there. Also that the window was wide open, a pair of white satin pumps lay on the plank floor like cast dice, and one of her dresser drawers was wide-open from where she'd hastily grabbed the clothing she'd run away in. Finally, his gaze landed on the wedding gown hanging on the back of the open closet door, beautiful, but lacking a bride.

"Well I'll be damned," he said at last. "She bolted."

"Eric, I'm so, so sorry."

He stuck his head out the open window as though he might catch Ashley outside. But she was long gone. He drew himself back into the room. His gaze burned into hers. "Did you actually see her leave?"

She nodded her head. "Yes."

"Did she leave alone?"

Oh, God, why hadn't she stayed with the other brides-maids? There was a pause. She swallowed. She couldn't lie. "No."

He sank down on Ashley's bed. "This is a disaster."

He sounded so dejected. She tried to put things in perspective to bolster him up. "Well, not a disaster in the classic sense. It's not the sinking of the Titanic. It's not a plague of locusts destroying the food supply, it's not a tsunami roaring up Malibu beach dragging everything into the blue sea. It's not," she stretched her imagination, trying to think of a disaster so extreme that this would seem minor, "the zombie apocalypse."

His expression was bleak and hopeless. "Yeah, it is."

"Come on, Eric. Maybe she just got cold feet." She was

actually kind of surprised that his reaction was this extreme. He'd always been so laidback during the wedding planning that she had begun to wonder if he was as passionately in love with Ashley as a man on the brink of marriage ought to be.

"You don't get it," he said.

Okay, she didn't get it, but what she did get was that there were a couple hundred guests who needed to be informed that today's ceremony would not be going ahead as planned. "Maybe we should go get, I don't know, Duncan Carnarvon?" And she definitely didn't want to be the one who had to deliver the bad news to Ashley's uncle. "Or maybe Millicent Carnarvon is the best person to deal with this?" He hadn't changed his expression at all. She tried again. "What about your mother?"

As though she had summoned the woman, Grace Van Hoffendam suddenly appeared in the bedroom doorway, a vision of elegance in a blue silk suit, matching pumps, white gloves, and a jaunty hat perched over her freshly-coiffed hair. "What is going on?" she asked. "Everyone is getting restless, the chamber orchestra had to start their set over again. The ice sculptures are melting."

When she didn't get a reply from either of them she glanced around, took in the disarray in the room, and walked jerkily toward the open window. She stuck her head out, turned to the right and then to the left, then pulled herself back into the room to stare at the two of them as understanding dawned. "Oh my God. She didn't."

"Yeah, Mom, she did," Eric said.

Then, Grace Van Hoffendam, the most elegant society woman that Tasmine had ever seen, did a very strange thing. She walked up to where the dress hung against the back of the door, its full skirt billowing. She drew back her fist and she punched the dress.

Tasmine was so shocked she didn't know what to say. Clearly, reciting all the things that would be worse than a runaway bride, everything from the sinking of the Titanic to the zombie apocalypse, was not going to cut it with Eric's mother. She got the sense that no one ever rejected the Van Hoffendams. All her sympathy had been with Eric and his mom, but when Grace hauled back and punched the dress, she began to wonder.

However, whatever the outcome of this wedding, she had been hired both as a bridesmaid and as a wedding coordinator. She imagined she was going to have to be the wedding un-coordinator and somehow get rid of the guests with the least fuss possible.

As gently as she could, she said, "I think someone needs to make an announcement that the wedding is not going to go ahead. Do you want me to talk to Mr. Carnarvon?"

Grace stared at her for an unseeing moment. "You're absolutely certain Ashley's gone?"

Tasmine didn't feel like sharing with Grace that she had helped Ashley scramble out of her wedding gown and into street clothes. She didn't share that she had watched Ashley jump into the driver's seat of an expensive Italian convertible beside the sexiest screenwriter in LA. She didn't share that Ashley had exchanged a passionate kiss with Bennett Saegar right before she jammed her foot on the gas and fled from her own wedding. All she said was, "Yes, I'm sure she's gone."

Grace's hands formed fists, and Tasmine moved unconsciously in front of the poor dress to protect it from further violence. She could see a vein pulsing in Grace's neck beneath a fat string of pearls. Her impeccable blue silk suit, matching pumps and straw hat made an incongruous background for the rage suffusing her face.

"No," she snapped. "This is our son's wedding. My husband will say everything that needs to be said."

"Okay. Would you like me to go and get him?"

For a moment she thought that Grace would nod her head and relinquish the unpleasant task to Tasmine, but suddenly the small woman drew her shoulders back. "No. A bridesmaid rushing up to him will only cause comment. If his wife goes and sits beside him, that will seem perfectly natural. I'll explain the situation, and Charles will make a short announcement."

Eric glanced up. "Do you want me to come with you, Mom?"

Graces lips thinned in an angry line. "No. The best thing you can do is stay quietly out of sight." She turned to Tasmine. "That little tramp was never good enough for my son, or my family." Then she snapped, "Your job is to keep him out of sight."

She nodded. She understood that Grace was snapping orders because she was upset, but it was interesting how during the whole run-up to the wedding, even though she was distantly related to the Van Hoffendams, Grace had never let her forget that she was hired help.

Grace walked to the dressing table where a scatter of makeup and hairbrushes littered the surface. For a second Tasmine thought she was going to fix her makeup or comb her hair or something, then she realized Grace was staring down at Ashley's engagement ring. The ring had belonged to Grace. With shaking fingers, Eric's mother picked up the ring and pushed it onto the ring finger of her right hand. Then she stalked out of the room.

After his mother left, Eric looked so devastated she had to fight the urge to put her arms around him and offer him comfort. She heard the front door shut with a bang as his mother left to deliver the bad news to Charles Van Hoffendam.

She settled herself on the bed, a couple of feet away from where Eric sat staring at the floor. "I am so sorry. You must really love her." And maybe if Ashley could see him like this, she'd see what she was throwing away.

When Eric gazed up at her, it wasn't heartbreak she saw in his eyes. It was despair. He shook his head. "You don't understand. If I don't marry Ashley Carnarvon, I'm going to jail."

CHAPTER 2

"*J*ail?" She stared at Eric in stunned disbelief. Sure, he had a reputation for being a wild child and a playboy. The youngest son of the prestigious family, Eric seemed to be prolonging his adolescence as long as he could. He wasted a lot of his time and his family's money and he'd rather party than do anything useful, but what could he have done that would threaten jail? And why would marrying Ashley Carnarvon help? "Did you do something to Ashley?"

His expression was shocked when he said, "No!"

"Well then, what happened? And what does Ashley escaping out that window have to do with you going to jail or not?" She was so confused she felt like her head might explode. Her makeup, camera-ready on this special day, felt suddenly like plastic wrap on her face. The dress that was designed for waltzing up and down an aisle pinched her ribs when she sat on the bed. Even her shoes felt too small.

Eric heaved a deep sigh. "I might as well tell you. Everybody will know soon enough." He dropped his head in his hands. "Oh God, the media. My family will be so humiliated."

"Did you kill someone?"

Once more he gave her that shocked expression. "No!"

"Well, it can't be worse than that," she said practically.

"Okay." He held up a hand. "Don't start with the plagues of locusts and zombies again. I'll tell you." Then he paused as though trying to figure out where to start. She waited patiently until he said, "You know how sometimes I drink too much?"

"Oh, yes." She'd seen him more than a little inebriated at a couple of the pre-wedding events. Still, he was a happy drunk. She'd been very careful to quietly ensure he didn't get behind the wheel of a car, but had soon realized he never drove if he was going to be drinking so she didn't imagine he'd crashed his car or anything.

"Well, this one night I got totally wasted. Me and some buddies were partying." He looked at her, and she saw the puzzle-ment in his eyes. "I don't know what came over us. My buddy has these neighbors, real stick-up-their-ass people, friends of the Carnarvons. We were pissed to the gills and somehow ended up on their property. My buddy decided that we were going to call on them and get them to invite us in for a drink. And yes, we were drunk enough that this seemed like a possibility."

He blew out a breath. "They weren't there. One thing led to another and we accidentally broke into their house."

Her eyes opened so wide she felt her hairspray cracking. "You broke into someone's house? Are you out of your mind?"

"Yes. That's what I'm telling you. We were completely out of our minds. We were looking for more booze. Swear to

God, that's all we wanted. Well, we got inside, and my buddy started looking for their booze cabinet. We figured it would be in the living room where they do all their entertaining. So they have these pictures on the walls. You know, Picasso type stuff."

She was getting a sick feeling. "You mean priceless works of art?"

His gaze was bleak when he glanced up at her. "We never should have been there."

She felt as though she were with them in that room; Eric, off-his-face drunk, a couple of other entitled rich boys, equally pissed. "So, you found the booze?"

He stared at his shoes as though admiring the shine. "No. I found a Sharpie."

She was getting a really bad feeling about a story that included Picasso type art, drunkenness and an indelible marker. She didn't want to hear what happened next, but she had to know. "Go on."

"I grabbed the pen. I was doing an impression, like I was an art instructor. The guys were doubled over laughing. I was waving the pen around and then I added a pair of boobs to one of the paintings."

She had a wild impulse to laugh. But that's what had got Eric into all this trouble. People laughed at his pranks too easily. "Tell me it wasn't a real Picasso."

He shook his head. "But it was someone famous, and even worse, Judge Bailey's wife knew the artist or something and she brought the painting over all the way from Paris. I think, if we'd only helped ourselves to the booze and peed in the pool, the judge would have let us go."

She let her disgust show in her tone when she said, "You peed in their pool?"

He didn't raise his eyes from contemplation of his shoes. Merely nodded.

She was still confused about the Ashley part. "So, was Ashley there?" Ashley might be a little unconventional herself, but Tasmine couldn't imagine her condoning this behavior.

He shook his head impatiently. "No. The Baileys have a security company. I barely got the second nipple on the painting when the rent-a-cops showed up. There wasn't much we could say. They had security cameras everywhere. Next thing, my parents are there. It's all kind of fuzzy, but the next day, I got to watch a video of me acting like a jackass on the footage from the security cameras. I had to watch it in front of my parents, the Baileys, the cops, and with a hangover you wouldn't believe."

Now that he'd started, he seemed to want to finish his confession. "The judge was yelling, and Mrs. Bailey just cried, quietly, you know? Like when someone dies? My dad, of course, said they'd pay for everything. Get the pool drained, send the painting to the greatest art restorers in the world. But it wasn't enough. Judge Bailey said he was pressing charges. Breaking and entering, vandalism, he listed off a bunch of charges. And him being, you know, a judge, would not go well for me."

She could picture the scene so clearly. Even though she didn't know the victims, she couldn't help but say, "Poor Mrs. Bailey."

"Yeah. I think that's what made the judge so rabid. It was his wife's crying. But not even mad crying, more like her heart was broken."

"I bet she has no kids. I bet those pictures are like her family."

He didn't seem to hear her. "So, we went home, and my dad talked to our lawyers, and, I don't even know who came up with the idea. My mom, I think. But I've been hanging out with Ashley for, like, ten years. It was never super serious, but my dad and mom thought that since the judge and the Carnarvons are so tight and, you know," he made air quotes here, "she's a good girl from a good family, that if I was getting married to Ashley Carnarvon, there was no way Judge Bailey would send me to jail."

He scuffed the floor of Ashley's bedroom like a little kid. "Well, it worked. I asked Ash to marry me, she said yes, and then my dad talked to the judge. He said that so long as I married Ash, got a real job, and the pool and the painting were restored, he'd drop the charges."

"Did Ashley know about this?"

"No. We didn't want anyone to know."

Were the Van Hoffendams for real? Were they seriously so entitled that they thought they could play with people like pawns? "I cannot tell you how much of a horrible idea this was on every level. How could you begin marriage with a woman based on self-preservation? A woman you don't even love."

"I do love Ashley. Kind of. She's a good friend, she's been around forever."

"No. That's not love. Love is for grown-ups who know how to give without always taking." She was so mad she got up and started to pace. She didn't even understand the source of her anger. It wasn't like this was even her business, except that somehow it was. The minute Ashley had passed her that wedding dress, she'd somehow taken responsibility for the runaway bride. And the fallout. An overdeveloped sense of responsibility, that was her problem.

"Yeah, well, anyway, that's the story. Without this marriage, I'm screwed."

There wasn't much she could say, because it looked as though he was right.

She stayed with Eric for the next hour. She went to the kitchen and brewed a pot of coffee for something to do. She had promised Grace Van Hoffendam that she would stay with her son until further notice, and that's what she did. She'd intended to earn her money by being part of a great wedding, now she seemed to be earning it by babysitting the jilted groom. A man she didn't have a lot of respect for at the moment.

There wasn't much food in the fridge but she made them sandwiches out of cheese, a loaf of organic bread she found in the freezer, and a slightly wrinkled tomato. Eric barely noticed; he ate the sandwich she put in front of him, he drank his coffee, and she did the same. They waited. On their second cup of coffee, the three bridal parents showed up. Ashley's mom had tear streaks down her pretty face. Grace had the blank look of a woman who's just downed half a dozen tranquilizers, and Charles Van Hoffendam's face could have been carved of granite. Gray, hard, implacable. He glared at Tasmine. "The wedding's canceled and the other bridesmaids have gone home. I think you'd better leave, too."

Eric stood up when his father came in the room. "Doesn't matter, Dad. I told her everything."

"Then you'd better tell her to keep her mouth shut. We're getting in the car and we're driving straight to Judge Bailey's home. We have to get there before he hears the gossip. Half the people at this ceremony are friends of his. He'll know you've been jilted within the hour." He banged one fist into his open palm. "How could she do this to us?"

Ashley's mom wiped her wet cheeks. "I'm so sorry. It's not like Ashley. I don't understand it." Then she lifted her head. "Judge Bailey?" She sniffed. "He didn't even come to the wedding."

Grace sent her cool look. "I'll explain everything later. For now, my husband is right, we have to go and see the judge."

"Come along, son."

She counted the seconds until they were all out of there so she could get back into her street clothes, head home, and wash this makeup off her face and the hairspray out of her hair. And seriously rethink her future as a bridesmaid for hire.

"Wait," Eric said. "Tasmine has to come with us."

"A bridesmaid who couldn't manage the simple task of getting the bride to the wedding?" Charles snapped.

"We need her," Eric insisted.

Oh, she did not want to go to Judge Bailey's house. No, no, no.

His father looked at Eric as though he could not believe he'd sired such a cretin. "This is not the time to be dragging another girl to the judge. Do you think he's going to let you switch brides?"

"Oh, like that's an option," she snapped, seriously riled that this man thought she'd be available. Or interested.

Eric said, "She's our witness. She's the only person who actually saw Ashley run away. She can prove it wasn't my fault we didn't get married."

Charles stared through narrowed lids at his son, then slowly nodded. "I see what you're getting at. You stuck to your end of the bargain. When the judge hears that you got ditched at the altar, he might go easier on you." With a jerk of his chin to her, Charles said, "All right. You'd better come."

She'd had about enough of these people and their high-handed ways. "No, really, I don't think that would be a good idea."

Grace sent her a chilly look. "You were hired to be a bridesmaid and assist us in getting Ashley Carnarvon and my son married. You were the only one who could have stopped Ashley and you didn't. Frankly, I think the least you can do is help salvage this disaster. As far as I'm concerned, you are still on the clock."

Tasmine had put up with a lot. She'd hung around with Eric while he'd come to terms with the fact that he'd been ditched, she'd listened to a confession that made her furious that anyone with so many natural talents as Eric Van Hoffendam would waste his time on booze and pranks. It was time for him to grow up. And it was time for his parents to stop treating him like a baby. She was about to tell Grace and Charles exactly what she thought, when Eric touched her shoulder. "Of course you don't have to come. You've done a lot for us today and I really appreciate it. But if you could come with us and explain to the judge and his wife what you saw, it might help me stay out of jail."

His eyes were so sad, so sincere, so damn blue, like the Delft pottery from Holland where his ancestors had left to make their fortune in America. She did not want to be pulled into spending one more second with the Van Hoffendams, but she couldn't resist the naked appeal in his eyes. She nodded briskly. "I'll go change into my own clothes."

"But—"

Whatever Grace wanted to say, she wasn't listening. She said, "Give me ten minutes." And if they chose not to wait, that was absolutely fine with her.

For some reason, everyone was still in Ashley's bedroom. She said, "Why don't you wait for me out in the main room?"

It was Ashley's mom who shooed everybody out front. As she closed the bedroom door, Tasmine heard Melody Carnarvon ask once more, "I don't understand what Judge Bailey has to do with this. What is going on?"

As she swiftly changed from her bridesmaid dress back into her street clothes, Tasmine wondered whether Ashley had really been as clueless as Eric believed. Ashley might pretend to be a careless wild child, but she had discovered, from working with her as a bridesmaid, that there was a lot more to Ashley than she advertised.

She hoped the runaway bride would be happy. When she pulled up the last memory she had of her, throwing herself into Ben Saegar's arms and then laughing as she drove away, Tasmine had a pretty good feeling that Ashley was going to be just fine.

Eric, on the other hand, she wasn't so sure about.

CHAPTER 3

*S*he took the full ten minutes to get herself changed and to check messages on her phone. There was a one-word text message from Ashley that simply said, *Sorry!!!* Shaking her head, she dropped her phone back into her bag.

She glanced at that gorgeous dress all ready for a wedding that wouldn't happen.

Then, with about as much enthusiasm as she'd have if she was about to face final exams she hadn't studied for, she walked out into the other room.

The Van Hoffendams hadn't left. They were waiting in the main room of the cottage, all of them stiff in their formal wear. The four of them piled into Charles Van Hoffendam's Lincoln. Eric's father said, "Let me do the talking." Other than that, they listened to some god-awful classical music and were mostly quiet on the way to the judge's house. The air-conditioning was too chilly and Tasmine felt goosebumps rise on her arms, but she didn't feel like asking them to turn it down. They drove to Manhattan Beach and pulled into an absolutely stunning Spanish-style estate with a red tile roof.

She wondered if the Baileys would even be home. It was a beautiful, sunny Saturday afternoon; they could be out golfing, visiting friends, maybe they'd taken a picnic to the beach, were at a concert, a wedding, a funeral. Some servant would answer the door and send them away, and she could go home and forget all about the Van Hoffendams. But, after Eric's father rang the bell, a young woman in a navy skirt and white blouse answered the door. It was a kind of maid's uniform without the frilly apron. "Yes, sir?" she asked as she glanced at the four of them.

"We're here to see Judge Bailey. I phoned ahead. It's Charles Van Hoffendam and his family."

"Yes, sir, you're expected."

Tasmine couldn't identify the young woman's accent, but she thought it was Eastern European. Polish maybe.

The interior of the house was cool and hushed as though not a lot of action went on inside. The maid said, "Please come this way." She then led them forward down the quiet corridor and towards the back of the house. Eric grew increasingly uncomfortable as they went deeper inside, and she really couldn't blame him. He'd broken into this couple's home and vandalized their property. She was glad he at least had this much conscience.

When they entered the big room where the judge and his wife waited for them, she understood exactly why he was so flustered. This was clearly the main living room. It was a lovely room, formal yet comfortable, with the kind of chairs that a person could actually relax in. But the most amazing thing about the room was the art on the walls. Tasmine was no art expert, but she felt as though she were walking into a private art gallery. On the main wall were two Cubist paintings. It was obvious that a third painting that should sit between them was missing. The blank space in this wall of art looked like a beautiful smile missing a front tooth.

"Come in and sit down," commanded an older man, sitting in a high backed chair. He did not rise to greet them. Beside him, sat an elegant woman with a soft face. Even with her wrinkles and white hair, it was obvious that she had once been a very beautiful woman. There was a moment of uncertainty, and then Charles Van Hoffendam chose a seat near the judge. His wife sat beside him. She and Eric ended up sharing a loveseat across from his parents. She wondered if the judge had chosen the seating arrangement deliberately, and suspected he had. They looked up towards the top of the room where he and his wife sat side-by-side, very much where a judge would sit in a courtroom.

Judge Bailey did not have the softness of his wife. His face was calm but implacable, his jaw set. When she looked into his cool gray eyes, she imagined that he had seen and heard more of the ugly side of human nature than she could ever imagine. He did not look as though he would be easily moved to sympathy.

"We've got some bad news," Eric's father began.

The judge nodded. "Does this news have anything to do with the fact that your son, who is supposed to be getting married today, is sitting in our house instead of dancing with his new bride?"

Oh boy, he was not going to make this easy. Even though Charles Van Hoffendam must be used to dealing with tough customers all day long in his business, she could see him fidget. "The wedding did not go forward. We wanted to tell you in person, you and your wife, that my son stood up to his promises. He waited at the altar with every intention of marrying Ashley Carnarvon. But, she abandoned him there."

A clock ticked somewhere. It was a big tick. She imagined a grandfather clock, but she didn't turn her head to look. Her stomach was churning with anxiety. She couldn't even imagine what Eric was going through.

"Smart girl," the judge said.

There was utter silence in the room for a moment. She could see that Eric's father had no idea what to say. He couldn't agree with the judge without admitting that his son was a terrible bet for bridegroom, and he couldn't argue with the judge given the reason they were here.

Judge Bailey spoke again. "It went against my better judgment to allow your son to get off scot-free in the first place." His voice toughened. "He and his hooligan friends fouled our pool, they broke into our home, and then your son vandalized an irreplaceable painting." He turned his fierce and terrifying gaze on Eric. "Worse, the worst crime of all, you made my wife unhappy."

She waited for Eric to say something, but he sat there mute. It was his father who spoke once again. "And we are very, very sorry." He opened his mouth to go on but the judge spoke again.

"You told me that your son was preparing to marry a nice young woman from a good family. Only under those circumstances did I agree not to press charges."

She jabbed Eric sharply with her elbow. "Say something," she whispered urgently.

She saw him nod and then swallow. "Judge, Mrs. Bailey, I am so sorry for what I did. I know I can't fix the painting, but I wish I could go back and act differently."

The judge leaned forward, his penetrating gaze fixed once more on Eric. "No. You can't fix the painting. In fact, you can't fix any of this. You left it all to your father and mother and to me and I think it's time you were taught a lesson young man. I will be calling the police, and I will be pressing charges." He gave each of them in turn a piercing look, pausing on her for a moment as though puzzled as to why she was there. "Good day to you, the maid will see you out."

All three of the Van Hoffendams rose stiffly.

She couldn't believe this was it. Eric was spoiled, entitled and rich, but he wasn't a criminal. Before she was aware she was going to speak, her mouth opened and words came out. "Wait," she said.

She could not believe she was interfering. But how could they not see, all of these intelligent people, what was so obvious to her. Eric acted like an overgrown kid because that's how everyone treated him. Maybe she didn't know him all that well, but she thought that he was capable of a lot more than what he was offering the world. And she did not think that spending time behind bars was going to help him grow up.

Besides, Judge Bailey might be a judge but Charles Van Hoffendam wasn't a nobody. She imagined there would be lawyers and court dates and extensions and whatever legal maneuvers very rich, connected people could pull. None of which was going to help Eric. Now that she'd burst into speech, everyone turned to look at her.

She addressed the judge. She knew she couldn't make matters any worse, and she thought maybe there was a chance she could help a man who, even though she wanted to smack him upside the head, she was fond of.

She said, "I'm not rich like all of you people, I grew up in a family where if you wanted something, you worked for it. And if you screwed up, you worked hard to fix it. My mom and dad always said that the punishment should fit the crime. What will Eric learn from prison? How will it make him grow up and be a better man? When we broke something or messed up, we always had to fix it."

The judge stared at her for a moment. "Are you suggesting Eric take up art restoration?" He asked dryly. Okay, he was being sarcastic, but he was listening.

She shook her head. "Of course not. But that's not all Eric did. I bet there's pool maintenance and garden chores you need doing."

"My dear young lady, we have staff for that."

She felt a little desperate, but she'd opened her mouth, she felt like she needed to finish. "Okay, but there must be other jobs, maybe something really gross and dirty, that even your hired help doesn't want to do. I mean, if this was a farm, you could make him shovel out the pigpen."

She saw the gleam of something that might have been amusement cross the judge's face. They all waited for many seconds until he spoke again. "Well, now that the pool has been drained, it does need every inch of it scrubbed and repainted." He turned to his wife. "But, I'm not sure Martha would even allow him on the property."

Tasmine began to feel hopeful. The judge was an old tyrant, but his wife had a gentle, soft look. If there was ever a woman who was given to second chances, she suspected it was Mrs. Bailey.

After a moment, Mrs. Bailey said, "I'm never in favor of prison, if it can be avoided. I've always felt that many a criminal could be redeemed. I think this young lady has proposed a very sensible solution. We could look on this as community service hours in lieu of jail time. What do you think, Ernest?"

"There'd be no slacking," the judge warned. "If I were presiding over this case, I would sentence a hooligan like this to six months behind bars. If I commute the sentence, it will be to six months of hard physical labor." He held up a bony finger and pointed to Eric. "You will arrive at seven every morning, you will do every job you're given, and the gardeners, the cleaners, anyone on my staff has the right to give you work, the dirtier the better." He nodded. "It's not a bad idea." He glared at Eric, "Have you ever done any kind of physical labor?"

Eric looked as though he thought prison might be a better option. He shook his head, "No, sir."

"I think this young lady has a workable option. What do you think, Charles?"

She could tell that Charles was torn between hope that his son wouldn't have to go to jail and horror that anyone would make a Van Hoffendam scrub out their pool. But he didn't have a lot of options. "It's very good of you to keep my son out of the penal system."

The judge now shook his bony finger at Eric. "You will work long days, and they will be difficult. If I see any slacking, any tardiness, any sign whatsoever of alcohol, I will have my very good colleague the chief of police over here within minutes to put you in cuffs. Have I made myself clear?"

Eric nodded again. "Yes, sir."

The judge turned once more to his wife. "Martha? Are you sure about this?" She knew he was tough as an old boot, but it was sweet how much he cared for his wife. That had to count for something, had to mean there was softness somewhere in the old tyrant.

"I agree."

Eric's father cleared his throat. "Well. I'm glad that's settled."

As they were walking out of that art gallery of a room, the judge suddenly said, "Young lady?"

Tasmine was fairly certain he was referring to her. She turned. "Yes, Judge?"

"Who are you?"

"I'm Tasmine Ford, a distant cousin of the Van Hoffendams. And Eric's friend."

The old man nodded. "He needs more friends like you." He looked at her for a moment and said, "And you'd vouch for him, would you? You believe he is capable of hard work and responsibility?"

Did she? He'd shown no sign of responsibility and she'd never see him do a lick of work. But, some instinct within her believed there was more to Eric than he'd so far demonstrated. "Yes. I do."

"Good. Then, since this was your idea, I'm going to suggest you take the role of, let's say, parole officer."

She glanced at the old man with horror. "Parole officer?"

"I need someone I can call if he doesn't show up on time, or does shoddy work."

Grace spoke for the first time. "Surely, Judge, his parents are the people you should call."

"No. I like this young lady." He glanced shrewdly at Eric. "And I suspect your son will take her more seriously than he does you." Then, as though they were all in agreement, he said, "Leave your contact details with the maid."

. . .

I<small>F</small> T<small>ASMINE</small> <small>HAD</small> for one moment imagined she'd be receiving any thanks for saving Eric from jail, she was soon set right. No sooner were the four of them back in the car than Grace broke out into speech as though she could not contain her indignation one more second. "How could they do that to us?" she exclaimed. "That is such a humiliation. Making our son clean out their damn pool? Telling him he has to take orders from their hired help? Why, most of them probably don't even speak English!"

"He's power-hungry," Eric's father continued the tirade. "That's the problem. He's old and he'll soon be off the bench. He had the chance to lord it over us and there was nothing we could do about it. Well, he may be a powerful man in his world, but I am a powerful man in mine. I'm going to have a word with my lawyers. We'll see what we can do to scotch this nonsense."

They continued on in that vein for most of the drive home. Tasmine kept her mouth shut, and so did Eric. Charles Van Hoffendam was so busy thinking up all the ways he was going to humiliate Judge Bailey when he got the chance that they were nearly back at their mansion before she realized he had forgotten to drop her off at the Carnarvon estate where she'd left her car. She turned to Eric, sitting beside her in the backseat, "I need to get my car, it's at the Carnarvons."

He glanced at his father and shook his head. "Sorry about that, I'll drive you."

She imagined it would be kind of painful for him, driving back to the place where he was supposed to have married today, but on the other hand, she didn't have money for a cab and even if no one acknowledged the fact, she had saved him from prison. So she nodded. "Thanks."

When they reached their home, and everyone piled out of the car, Charles looked surprised to see her emerge from his backseat. He peered at her for a moment. "You'll be wanting a cab. I'll get the housekeeper to call one for you."

Eric came around the car and stood beside her. "Don't worry about it, Dad. I can drive her home."

And so, she soon found herself sitting beside Eric in his car, on his wedding day. He'd taken the time to run into the house and throw on some jeans and a sweatshirt, but he still had that just-barbered look.

They drove in silence for a few minutes. He had music on, Ed Sheeran she thought, but the sound was too low to be certain.

She was fantasizing about getting home, having a long, hot shower to wash away all the memories of this day.

After a while, he said, "There's something I want to say to you."

She rolled her eyes. "Don't tell me, you are so humiliated that you are actually going to have to do some hard, physical work for a change." She turned to him, suddenly furious about the way she'd been dragged into a mess not of her making, and the way she'd put yourself out for him and his family, and all they'd done was complain all the way home. She was angry that someone with so much potential, and so many advantages, was throwing them all away. She jabbed his arm with her fingernail, manicured just yesterday to match the color of her dress. "Well, let me tell you, I am sick of this whining. I am sick of you and your parents and your entitled attitudes about life. Who do you think you are? You strut around, and everything is so easy for you. You're gorgeous, entitled, rich and this is the best you can do with your life? I for one don't think you have been humiliated nearly enough. And I also think Judge Bailey did you a huge favor."

She crossed her arms over her chest and turned to stare out the window. The motion of the car changed and before she realized what was happening he'd pulled over onto one of the many viewpoints along the highway. She had an Alfred Hitchcock moment where she wondered if he was going to yank her out of the car and toss her over the cliff. But, to her surprise, he said, "What I wanted to say, is thank you. You were a good friend to Ashley. And you've been a good friend to me. I don't know where you got that idea, but if it wasn't for you, I would be going to jail."

She felt a little foolish now about her outburst. She said, "Okay. I'm glad somebody noticed that I saved your ass back there."

"Oh, I noticed. And my parents know it too. They're just used to getting everything they want," he said with a trace of bitterness, and she wondered if he felt that he was disappointing them.

He didn't pull the car back onto the highway right away. Instead, he said, "Was it the screenwriter?"

She was so surprised that he'd actually said thank you, that for a second she wasn't sure what he was talking about. "I beg your pardon?"

"When Ashley ran off. Was she with the screenwriter?"

She could lie, or she could refuse to answer, but he was going to find out the truth sooner or later. "Yes. She was."

He nodded. "I should have taught her to drive."

"What?"

"Ashley. The screenwriter was teaching her how to drive. That's how they started spending all their time together. I'm just saying, I should have taught her to drive."

Of course, on top of that horrible interview with the judge and his wife, he had been jilted at the altar today. "I'm really sorry she ran out on you like that. Are you going to be okay?"

"Sure. It's been a lousy day." Then he grinned at her for a heart-stopping moment. "But on the upside, you think I'm gorgeous."

She was still spluttering and he was still laughing when they pulled back onto the highway.

CHAPTER 4

*A*fter Eric dropped her off at her car, Tasmine longed to jump behind the wheel and drive back to her comfy apartment, enjoy that long, hot shower, throw on her pajamas, and find something to read or watch. Preferably a story that had nothing at all to do with weddings.

She had parked, when she'd arrived this morning, at the back of the cottage. She saw the lights on inside and imagined that Melody Carnarvon was inside alone. This was nothing to do with her, but again with the overdeveloped sense of responsibility. She'd check on Ashley's mom and make sure she was okay. That was the decent thing to do.

She knocked on the front door. Inside, she could hear music. John Mayer. Excellent music for crying to. She knocked again. She got the feeling that Melody was peeking out a window somewhere, checking out who was on the front porch. She waited and the door opened a minute later. With an internal sigh she realized she had guessed correctly. Melody's eyes were red-rimmed, and her face had the chapped look that suggested tears had fallen faster than she could wipe them away. She said, "I am so sorry."

Melody nodded and motioned her to come inside. "You want some hot chocolate? I was about to make some."

No one had offered her anything to eat or drink since she had made that pot of coffee and the sandwiches what seemed like hours ago. If she'd been offered alcohol she would've refused knowing if she drank anything stronger than tea she'd probably start crying. But there was something so comforting about hot chocolate that she said, "Thank you. I would."

Like her, Melody still sported salon-styled hair, and even after the crying jag her makeup still looked professionally done. However, she'd replaced the apricot colored strapless cocktail dress that was her mother-of-the-bride outfit with black stretchy yoga pants and an oversized cotton T-shirt. Big fuzzy slippers covered her feet and made a shushing sound as she walked. Tasmine followed her into the kitchen.

"I guess, if you went with them to see the judge, that you know everything."

"Yes. I was so shocked . . ."

"Can you even imagine how I feel?" Melody had taken a copper-bottomed saucepan out of the cupboard and now she banged it onto the stovetop. "I went over to my brother and sister-in-law's, because I felt so awful about Ashley running away like that. And Duncan ended up telling me about that sick and terrible plan to marry Ashley to Eric in order to protect him from jail. How could he even think of such a thing? And without asking me, or Ashley?" She shook her head. Poured milk into the saucepan and turned on the heat. "I yelled at my brother like I have never yelled at anyone before.

He claimed that marrying Eric Van Hoffendam was a good way for Ashley to make something of herself. How is marrying some lowlife, vandalizing, criminal getting ahead in life?"

She dug a can of hot chocolate mix from inside a cupboard.

"Besides, he obviously has a drinking problem."

Tasmine had plenty of opportunity to study Eric over the past few weeks and she'd seen him drink too much, but only when his loser friends were around. She didn't believe he had a drinking problem. She thought his problem was boredom. "Have you talked to Ashley?"

"Of course I have. I phoned her and told her to come right home. But she says that she and Bennett Saegar are going to drive down to Mexico for a couple of weeks. He needs to do some more research on his screenplay." She shook her head once more. "She sounds so happy. How did I not see that she was falling in love with another man right under my nose? I mean, we've known Ben's family for years. He was working in the pool house and he was kind enough to teach Ashley to drive. She says they really got to know each other with the driving and, apparently, she was helping him with his screenplay. My Ashley, who works in a coffee shop, helping a Hollywood screenwriter. I guess you just can't tell with love."

"No. You can't." Melody dumped generous amounts of chocolate powder into two big, green pottery mugs and poured in the hot milk. She stirred vigorously. "Do you want whipped cream?" She opened the fridge and pulled out one of those cans of ready-made whipped cream. "I hardly ever indulge in high fat stuff, but this is an emergency."

Tasmine said, "Sure, why not?" She'd put in an extra long session at the gym tomorrow.

Melody sprayed so much whip cream over the top of the hot chocolate that it resembled an ice cream cone. Then she sprinkled chocolate powder over the top of that. She handed Tasmine one of the mugs and held hers up in a toast. "Well, cheers."

"Cheers," Tasmine said, and they clinked pottery mugs. There was no possible way to drink hot chocolate like this without getting whipped cream all over her nose and mouth, so she didn't worry about it. Neither did Melody, and they ended up giggling when they saw each other's faces. Melody fetched a couple of paper towels so they could wipe themselves off.

"Well, a good laugh feels as good as a good cry, and today I've had both."

"I know. And, while I know today was really hard, I have a feeling that Ashley is going to end up much happier with her screenwriter than she would have been with Eric."

"Oh, don't even get me started. That Eric Van Hoffendam is nowhere near good enough for my daughter. He's not good enough for any decent girl."

"I know." But she wondered if one day he might be.

They chatted for a while, about yoga and, strangely, about hair products since they both had long blonde hair in a climate that could be hard on long blonde hair. When her chocolate was all drunk and she was certain that Melody was going to be okay, she said, "Well, I'd better get going. I want to shower all this gunk off my hair and face before I go to bed."

"It was so nice of you to come and check on me. Thank you."

"You're welcome." And she grinned. "Since I was hired to

help coordinate this wedding, I feel a certain responsibility that the whole thing didn't happen."

"So completely not your fault." And then Melody jumped up. "Oh, could you do one more incredibly huge favor?"

Oh, please let them not put her in charge of returning all the thousands of gifts that had been arriving for the last few weeks. Surely Grace or Millicent had some kind of assistant or secretary who could take care of it. But it wasn't gifts on Melody's mind. She said, "Could you take the wedding dress? Millicent says she won't have it on the property. It was designed especially for the girl who was supposed to marry my nephew, Ted. They didn't end up getting married, so they passed the dress on to Ashley. And, well, you saw how that ended."

Melody got up and walked into Ashley's bedroom and flipped on the light. Tasmine followed. The wedding gown hung where she had left it earlier, billowing from its silk padded hanger on the open closet door. "But it's a beautiful dress. It's not the dress's fault that Ashley and Eric didn't end up getting married." She felt sorry for that gown, designed with a perfect wedding in mind. Just looking at it filled her with visions of twirling on a ballroom floor, of two gold rings, and a lifetime of happiness stretching ahead. "Besides, it's worth a lot of money."

"Not to me, it's not. But you could probably sell it online, or at a high-end resale place. I think you deserve a little extra for how hard you worked to make this wedding a success."

"Are you sure?" As someone who knew a lot about weddings, she knew how expensive an Evangeline original gown was and how difficult they were to come by.

"Yes, of course I'm sure." Then Melody sent her a quizzical

look. "Might there be a wedding in your future? Is there a special man in your life?"

She shook her head. "Only Henry. He's usually the delivery guy when I order my sushi."

"Well, a wedding dress is a good place to start."

"Yes. I guess so."

Melody helped her pack the wedding gown back into its silk garment bag with the logo that brides worldwide drooled over. "Here, take the shoes as well. I don't want any memories of this wedding."

She doubted that she and Ashley were the same shoe size, but she understood how Melody felt. How many times had she thrown away every item in her apartment that reminded her of the boyfriend she was no longer seeing? Even down to tossing a dress of hers that he'd said was his favorite.

When she carried the wedding gown out to her car, she hung it carefully from the hook in the backseat. As she drove home, she glanced at it occasionally in the rearview mirror and the white confection filled her with pleasure. It took her two trips to bring up the suitcase that she always took to weddings, which constituted her emergency supply cupboard, sewing kit and drug store all combined. It was amazing how predictably somebody in the wedding party would need a painkiller, a fresh pair of nylons, a tampon, a torn bit of lace stitched up, or a dab of spot remover. In the case, she also had a full makeup kit, hairspray, and a few things for the guys. Then there was her own bridesmaid dress and shoes to haul up. She left the wedding dress until last.

She brought it into the apartment, carrying the dress across the threshold as though it were a bride, and stood looking around her. Tasmine was California through and

NANCY WARREN

through. She believed in self-help books and seminars, yoga, that you are what you eat, and she fervently believed in the law of attraction. She was convinced that what she believed in and focused on happened. She felt she had enjoyed some career success using these techniques, and she didn't see why they wouldn't work with her love life.

It wasn't that she was in a huge hurry to get married, but she was already twenty-six, and she knew she wanted kids before she turned thirty. She also wanted to get married first, and have the kid after, no matter what the fashion was in L.A. So, instead of hanging that gorgeous dress up in the back of her closet somewhere, or taking it to a premier vintage store to try and get a few bucks, she thought that a wedding gown designed Evangeline was definitely the kind of item that could attract the right kind of energy. Hopefully, the right kind of partner.

She was reasonably good with simple handyman tools, since she worked selling high-end furniture, so it didn't take her long to figure out a way to hang the dress from her bedroom wall. She hung it on the wall opposite her bed, so it would be the first thing she looked at when she woke up in the morning, and the last thing she'd see when she went to bed.

She didn't have a lot of control over the Feng Shui of her apartment's location, but she did her best within the rooms and she liked to think that she'd set the dress up in her romance area. The shoes were entirely the wrong size so she added them to her emergency supply case knowing that one day a bride would snap a heel on her wedding day and Tasmine, the perfect bridesmaid, would once again fix the problem.

Just looking at that dress made her feel optimistic and somehow happy.

She enjoyed her long, hot shower, changed into her pajamas, and then crawled into bed. Instead of watching a movie, as she'd planned, she pulled out her journal. Law of attraction stated that you should always be very clear in your goal, and visualize it in rich detail. So, she opened her journal to a new page, and began to describe to herself her perfect wedding and her perfect man. She wrote with her favorite pen. It tracked purple ink in a smooth, flowing line as the image of her and this man grew substantial in her imagination. When she finished, she was surprised to find that an hour had passed. She read over what she'd written. The wedding was pretty romantic, but when she read the description of the bridegroom she'd visualized, she dropped her head in her hands. "Oh, no," she moaned aloud.

There were a ton of single men in California in her preferred age range. Why, of all of them, had she described perfectly Eric Van Hoffendam? A man who had not only been jilted that very day, but who was so far from grown-up that it might be years before he was mature enough to consider marriage. Besides, there was the other problem that he'd never looked at her as anything but a kind of buddy.

She was going to have to tear out these pages and visualize a completely new bridegroom. But tonight, she was simply too tired. She set the journal aside, enjoyed a last glance at the dress that hung on her wall like a promise. And then she flipped off her light and settled herself to sleep.

∾

ERIC LIKED POOLS. He tried to think of all the fun things he'd done in swimming pools. He'd learned to swim. He'd floated around on inner tubes and air mattresses, he'd dived into the cool blue deep, he'd played water polo, he'd had sex a time or two. And never, in all the time he'd spent floating atop, swimming through, or diving under the water had he thought that one day he might find himself scrubbing the surface of an empty pool on his hands and knees.

There were moments, when the sun beat down and he was convinced that the judge and Mrs. Bailey owned the largest swimming pool on the planet, that he really thought he'd rather be in jail. It wasn't only that every muscle in his body ached and squealed, it was the way they looked at him, like he was a criminal. The judge treated him with absolute contempt, while Mrs. Bailey always made sure he had plenty of water to drink, and did he have something to eat? The first day, it had never occurred to him that workers had to bring their own lunch, but he was too proud to say anything. By the end of the day he was so hungry he could have eaten off his own arm.

When he got home he blew off some friends who wanted to party, showered off the dirt and sweat and crashed into bed. The next morning, their cook found him yawning in the kitchen. "What are you doing?" she cried as he stood at the counter inexpertly slicing bread at an hour when he was usually either asleep or just getting home.

"Making a sandwich." Since there were no secrets from Millie, he said, "Working men pack their own lunches."

"Not when they're Van Hoffendams, they don't," she said, elbowing him aside. She didn't even ask him what he wanted.

She'd been with the family for years and knew his tastes as well as he did.

His second day on the job was pretty much a duplicate of the first. Except for two things that happened. First, he was scrubbing at a stubborn patch of algae, when a shadow fell over him. He turned his head and glanced up. Under the brim of his ball cap, he saw the judge staring down at him like the wrath of God. The old man didn't say anything and after a second Eric went back to work. A couple of hours later, he had his second visitor of the day. A female voice called down to him, "Hey, you missed a spot." He squinted up and Tasmine stood at the edge of the pool. Her hair hung in blonde curls over her shoulders and the way the sun hit, it sparkled like gold.

"Very funny. What are you doing here?"

She tossed something at him and he grabbed at it reflexively. It was a pair of work gloves. If she hadn't already identified herself as Tasmine, he would have thought that an angel of mercy had divined the blisters on his hands and come down to earth to spare him. "It's what all the hot working guys wear."

"Thanks."

He straightened and tried not to squeal like a girl from the pain in his back. He walked over to the silver ladder and climbed up and out of the pool. Tasmine looked cool and beautiful, like something out of a magazine. She wore a black and white skirt that showed off great legs, snappy black heels, and a crisp white shirt. There was something so tidy about her. She always seemed capable and put together, like a woman who not only had all the answers, but arranged them alphabetically. He waved the gloves. "How did you know?"

She had a little dimple when she smiled. Just one, on the left side of her face. "I have my ways."

"The judge?" He couldn't imagine Judge Bailey had bothered to arrange to get him some work gloves, but the judge was the only person he'd seen since he got here this morning.

She tilted her head to one side. "Don't get any ideas. I think the judge is a man who keeps all his tools in good working order. And if you end up with massive blisters, you won't be able to do the job."

"Point taken."

"Do you have plenty of water?"

"I do. I brought a gallon from home, and there's a garden hose on the property."

"Good." She glanced at the slim gold watch on her wrist. "It's almost lunchtime, do you have something to eat?"

"I do." He remembered how she used to run around after him when they were little kids. She didn't resemble too much the chubby little girl she'd been, but she still had a scatter of freckles across the bridge of her nose and up high on her cheeks. "I can't believe you took time out of your busy day to come and check on me."

She shrugged. "It's the middle of the day. I usually take a break around now anyway."

"Why don't you have lunch with me?" He gestured to where he'd left a small hiking backpack under the shade of a tree. "Millie, our housekeeper, insisted on packing the lunch. There's enough food in there to feed an army. You'd be doing me a favor if you shared it."

"I don't know." But she seemed as though she wasn't opposed to the idea.

"Think of it as part of your parole officer duties. You can

ask penetrating questions about my childhood, my criminal influences, my plans to stay straight."

He thought her laugh was one of the most charming things about her. It wasn't a high-pitched giggle like some girls, but sort of musical, and the notes lightened his mood. "And do you plan to stay straight?"

"If I have a good woman to help me."

She glanced around. "I can't sit on the grass."

Since the pool had been drained, somebody had piled all the pool furniture in a shed behind the pool house. "Got it covered." He picked up a small, wrought-iron table that reminded him of patios in the south of France, and two matching chairs. He set them up under the shade of the tree. Then he grabbed a sweatshirt out of his pack and used it to polish any possible dust off her chair.

"Thank you," she said, and sat down.

"Let me go wash my hands." He did, at the outdoor faucet, and then returned.

He dug out the enormous sack of lunch that Millie had packed him. "We've got ham on rye," he said, peering at one pack of sandwiches, "egg salad on brown, and either tuna salad or chicken salad on some kind of multigrain."

"You really weren't kidding. That is enough food for an army. Is it okay if I have the egg salad?"

He handed her the package of sandwiches along with a linen napkin. There was soda packed in ice to keep it cold, a slab of lemon cake, which Millie knew was his favorite, and two apples. He made Tasmine laugh while they ate, reciting his conversations with José, the head gardener. "He doesn't want me here. José has a plan to get rid of me."

She laughed her musical, tinkling laugh. "I think you're

getting sunstroke. Why would the head gardener want to get rid of you? If you don't scrub out that pool, he's going to have to do it."

"I'm telling you, he's got it in for me. When I talk to him he pretends he doesn't understand. He only ever speaks to me in Spanish. Fast Spanish, so I can't even catch a few words."

"Well, maybe he only speaks Spanish. Lots of people in California do."

"I heard him talking to Mrs. Bailey. He speaks English to her."

Her lips twitched. "Okay, that is suspicious."

As he realized that he could still make a pretty girl laugh, he began to think that maybe he did have a future after all. Maybe he would get out of this jail of his own making. But, of course he didn't tell her any of that. Instead, he passed her a slice of cake, and used his pocketknife to cut her apple into slices.

She only stayed maybe half an hour, but it was the highlight of his day. Not that that was saying much.

He'd had a lot of time to think as hour after hour passed and inch-by-inch he scraped and scrubbed. As they crunched on apples, he said, "I've been wondering why you spoke up that day. What made you think that the judge would go for the slave labor option instead of sending me to jail?"

Her brow wrinkled slightly as though she were puzzling about it herself. Finally, she said, "I think when you first told me the story, when we were sitting in Ashley's bedroom after she left, that it seemed to me he had wanted to go easy on you. I mean, he's a judge. He's used to sentencing criminals. It was obviously his first impulse, especially in the shock of what had happened and seeing his wife cry. But, after he calmed down, it seems like maybe your mom and dad gave him a way out by suggesting that you marrying Ashley Carnarvon was going to somehow rehabilitate you."

She leaned forward and he got a glimpse of that one winking dimple. "I mean, no offense, but Ashley's not exactly a star debutante. And if he knows the Carnarvons as well as I think he does, he was fully aware of that. So, once Ashley was no longer a viable excuse, I gave him another option."

"And you couldn't think of anything better than six months of hard labor?"

"My father always said that there was nothing like hard work and a good night's sleep to keep the devil at bay."

Eric thought about how exhausted he was at night and how he didn't have any energy or interest in raising hell anymore. "He might be onto something, at that."

She dusted her hands off on the red linen napkin and rose. "Thanks again for lunch. And please thank Millie."

"You're welcome. And thank you for the gloves, and the company."

Their gazes connected for a fleeting moment and he thought that if circumstances were different, he'd be very interested in going after this girl. But circumstances weren't different. She'd as good as told him he was an overgrown kid. He had a sneaking feeling she might be right.

When she stepped into the sunlight, he noticed that her nose and cheeks were sun-reddened. He stepped forward. "You got a little bit of a sunburn."

She put a hand to her cheek. "Oh, no. I was outside more than I thought I'd be today. I'll have to stop and buy some sunscreen, I left mine at home."

"I've got some." Once more, he had Millie to thank. He

rummaged in the pack and found a tube of sunscreen. Even though he'd given his hands a thorough wash before lunch, he wiped them once more on his napkin. Then he squeezed a dab of the rich cream onto the tip of his middle finger. He stepped forward and lightly spread the cream across the top of her cheekbone. He couldn't believe how soft her skin was, and how delicate. He was careful, restraining himself to the lightest touch. He traced the bridge of her nose and back down the other side to do her other cheek. As he gazed down at her, he caught the fresh scent of her, a blend of citrus and her own scent. Her eyes were blue-green and she had a mouth that looked perfect for kissing.

Ever since she'd become a bridesmaid for his wedding, he'd been used to her organizing things, issuing instructions, and making suggestions—usually sensible ones—to everyone involved. He thought of her as a nice woman, someone he'd immediately turned to when he had a question about what kind of gift he should give to his groomsmen, and whether he was supposed to give Ashley a wedding present.

There were so many things about getting married that he didn't know, it had been nice to have someone to turn to. But now, in the dappled shade of the tree, as he smoothed the cream into her soft, soft skin, he didn't think about how well organized she was, or how capable she was. He became obsessed with the idea of kissing her.

As though she felt his sudden desire through the tips of his fingers, her gaze suddenly rose and connected with his. For one perfect second he thought maybe she was feeling it too, and then she blinked. And stepped back out of his reach.

"Thank you. I don't want to get a sunburn, I hate it when my nose peels." She shook her head as though that wasn't what she'd meant to say, and it made him happy to see that this well-organized, always cool woman was suddenly flustered.

TASMINE HEADED BACK to her car, feeling that she was in danger of a lot worse than sunburn if she didn't watch herself around Eric. She felt flustered and far too aware of how appealing he could be. She'd adored him in formalwear but there was something about a guy who's been working hard physically that was pretty hot. He was probably acting interested because he was bored and she was on the premises, she reminded herself. She was also cynical enough to wonder if he'd hoped to get on her good side as she was his parole officer in the judge's eyes. She skirted the house and was walking down the path to where she'd parked when the judge called to her. She suspected he'd been watching for her.

"Miss Ford?"

"Tasmine, please," she answered automatically.

"May I speak to you for a moment?"

"Of course."

"You saw the perp?"

It was such an odd term from a formal man, like something you'd hear on a TV cop drama that she was surprised. "Yes. I gave him the gloves."

"I'll reimburse you. José, our gardener, was supposed to give him some but he claims there aren't any spare gloves on the entire property. Of course, he thinks Eric is a lazy gringo."

Because she had no idea how to answer, she didn't. Merely smiled.

"She came here, you know."

"Who did?"

"The young woman he was meant to marry. Ashley Carnarvon. She came with a young screenwriter friend who wanted some background from me on a screenplay he's writing."

"Really?" The sly old fox. "When was this?"

He appeared to be trying to remember when she suspected he knew to the minute when Ashley had been in his house. "It was a Sunday. Week before last, I think. They stayed for lunch."

"And did you happen to tell her about Eric and the painting?" She kept her tone neutral, but she wondered if he'd somehow arranged to get Ashley here for revenge.

"To be honest, I thought she knew. It was such a coincidence. Why would she, of all people, come to our house at such a time? Anyway, I thought she and the screenwriter were playing some kind of game. Foolish of me. My profession makes me see the worst in people. So, I was the one who told her about the vandalism. I showed her all the footage."

"Do you think it was the right thing to do?"

"I think she deserved to know what kind of man she was marrying, and if he was going to marry her then he should have told her himself. It's what an honorable man would do."

"I'm not sure either of you acted honorably," she said, with more honesty than tact.

He sighed. "That's my wife's opinion, too."

CHAPTER 5

*E*ric's days fell into a routine. He rose at dawn, dressed in his workingman's uniform of jeans and a T-shirt, stuffed his feet into old sneakers and set a ball cap on his head. He'd collect the lunch that Millie always left him in the fridge and loaded up a gallon of water. Millie had offered to make his breakfast for him, but she already had to do his mom and dad's breakfast every morning and he didn't see why he should add to her workload. Besides, he liked the quiet time to himself in the morning.

He put on coffee, made toast, usually scrambled himself some eggs, grabbed some fruit and he was out of there. He made certain to arrive at the Bailey's property well before his start time of seven. At first, it was out of fear that if he was so much as five minutes late the judge would haul him off to jail. After the first couple of days, the judge didn't bother to check on his arrival. But José did. He knew the head gardener had it in for him and he was determined not to give the guy an excuse to badmouth him to the judge or to Mrs. Bailey.

But, after a while, he realized he was arriving early as a

point of pride. He'd made a commitment to these people and damn it, he was going to stick to it.

The work was mind-numbingly tedious and physically exhausting. Even the endless tunes on his iPod got boring after a while. He started downloading podcasts on subjects that interested him, and then audiobooks. He'd never done very well in school, but it wasn't because he was stupid. It was because he was bored and lazy. But, as each day passed, and he took a small measure of pride in the section of pool he had cleaned so thoroughly that not even José could find anything to complain about, he started to get a sense of how much his laziness had cost him. He should have done better in college.

Maybe, if he'd put more effort into his education, he wouldn't have been so bored that he pulled stupid jokes and pranks. Maybe, if he'd tried harder in school, he'd have some idea about what he wanted to do with his life. He knew what he didn't want to do, and that was become a stockbroker. Even the small amount of studying he'd done so far had made him realize that he had zero interest in the world of stocks and bonds. He'd seen his stockbroker's license as a ticket to an easy life. But maybe an easy life wasn't much of a goal.

He was a physical guy, he liked to be active, preferably outside. He didn't want to spend his waking hours selling clients on some company that might improve its profits or might not, and he really didn't want to spend three-hour lunches courting people he didn't particularly like.

As the days went by, he had a lot of time to think, and he started to get a pretty clear idea of what he did not want in life. And what he didn't want was exactly where he was headed at the moment. But, his big problem was, if he changed course what direction was he going to take? Why was it so much easier to know what he didn't want to do than what he did?

It took him two weeks to finish the pool. As he scrubbed the last patch of algae off the final corner of the pool he felt a sense of pride. He stretched out on his back and took a break to suck back about a liter of water. Then he went looking for José. But before he found the head gardener, he bumped into Mrs. Bailey. She was cutting roses. As he walked by, he said "Good morning, ma'am."

She startled as though she hadn't heard him approaching, and he wondered whether she was losing her hearing. The only other possibility was that she was nervous of him, and it hurt him to imagine that might be true. He barely knew the woman, but he saw goodness in her that made him want her to like him, or at least not to be afraid of him. So, he paused and said, "It's a beautiful day." Since it was about day one hundred in a row of solid sunshine, and everyone was desperate for rain, he knew that it was a stupid thing to say. But the foolish comment was all he could come up with on the spur of the moment.

She glanced up at him from under the brim of a big straw hat and said, "Yes, it is."

Her gloved hand was closed around a pair of clippers, but he could see that she was struggling to cut through the thorny stems of the roses. Her hand shook. On impulse he knelt beside her and put his hand out for the clippers. He said, "Why don't you point out which stems you want and I'll cut them."

He saw her waver, and then decide to trust him. At least with a few rose stems. "Thank you. It's just this wrist is a little weak. I broke it a few years ago and it's never been quite right."

"No problem." He snipped and carefully placed the bloom in the shallow basket where three roses already lay. "Which one next?"

"That one, I think."

He grasped the stem of the pink bloom she was pointing to and cut it so it was about the same length as the others. She kept pointing and he kept clipping and in less than five minutes, there were more than a dozen pink and white roses in her basket.

"Thank you," she said. "That was very kind."

"Happy to do it." He stood and when he would have moved on, she said, "Are you getting on all right?"

He wasn't entirely sure what she meant by those odd words, but assuming she was referring to him working here he said, "Yes. I just finished scrubbing out the pool. I'm looking for José to let him know."

Maybe she heard the note of pride in his voice, for she said, "That's wonderful. I believe you'll find José down on the long lawn overlooking the ocean.

He walked down that way and sure enough José was there along with two other Mexican helpers. He walked up to the head gardener. "Hola," he said.

José fired something back in rapid Spanish and one of the other gardeners laughed. Eric didn't catch many of the words but he knew what gringo meant.

He was tired of being barked at in Spanish by a man who spoke perfectly good English. He drew from his pocket his secret weapon. A Spanish-English dictionary. If José wanted to play this game with him, he was perfectly willing to play along. He knew a little Spanish, but pretended to know none, he opened up the pocket dictionary and said aloud,

"Let's see, *I* . . ." He went through the book, then he said, "*Yo*," and pointed to himself. Then he muttered, "I have finished... f, f, f, there it is." He glanced up at José and said, "*Terminar.*"

The two Mexican helpers gazed at José, looking puzzled. They obviously knew he could speak English perfectly well. He glanced from one to the other of them, "Hey, if either of you guys speaks English, maybe you could translate?"

He knew all three of them had understood him when they exchanged glances and the two helpers merely shrugged as though they had no idea what he'd just said.

He turned back to his book, muttering, "Pool . . . pool." In another minute he managed to spit out, "*Yo terminar la piscina.*" He knew damned well that was wrong but a language barrier could work two ways.

José glared at him for a moment and then jerked his head. Eric was a head taller than the gardener and so to glare at him the man had to stare up. Eric could tell it annoyed him. Naturally, he drew himself up as tall as he possibly could, adding to the height difference.

José stomped ahead of him all the way to the pool. He climbed inside and walked around inspecting the work but Eric knew he'd done a great job and there was nothing to criticize. Naturally, this annoyed José even more. He muttered something in Spanish and then climbed out of the pool and strode to a small shed and threw open the door. Inside were pool chemicals, nets, life-saving devices, and on the shelf in the back was a collection including some large cans of paint. He hefted a five-gallon pail down and dumped it at Eric's feet, an inch from his toe.

Eric pulled out his dictionary once more. "How . . ." He

said aloud as he thumbed through the pages. "Como . . . Let's see. How do I apply it?"

José grabbed the dictionary out of his hand and tossed it in a trashcan in the corner. In flawless English, he said, "Follow the directions on the can. Rollers, handles, brushes, everything's in that corner there. You need something else, you ask me." Then, glaring one more time, he stomped back out of the pool shed.

Eric waited until he was gone before letting out his grin. It was only a small victory against the gnarly gardener, but it was a start.

He hefted the pail of paint and painting supplies to the edge of the pool and then read the directions.

No one had ever specified his hours. The judge had told him to arrive by seven every morning, but had never given a quitting time. So he set his own hours. He arrived a little before seven every morning, took around half an hour lunch break, and worked until about five.

He figured no one could accuse him of slacking with those hours, and he was keeping track of them, hoping he might get his sentence repealed early for good behavior.

He got set up, hauled everything into the pool, pulled out his iPod and set to work.

It was almost four o'clock when Tasmine caught his eye by waving down at him. He pulled out his earbuds. "Hi."

"Hi. I don't know what you're listening to, but I called your name twice and you didn't hear me."

"Sorry. I was listening to a podcast. I was concentrating, never even heard you." She wore a pretty blue sundress and heels. Big, dark, sunglasses shielded her eyes. "What you doing here?"

"I'm here on business. Mrs. Bailey wants to redecorate a couple of her upstairs rooms and asked me to quote on her furniture."

"Nice."

"I thought, since I'm here anyway, I'd come over and say hi."

"Hi."

"And also to ask if you can help me move a couple of heavy pieces of furniture out of the way."

"Sure."

He pulled a rag out of his back pocket and made sure his hands were clean and dry before climbing out of the pool. He and Tasmine walked toward the back of the house. They crossed an outdoor patio where the judge sat at a round glass and wrought-iron table with his newspaper spread out in front of him along with what looked like a gin and tonic and a tray of snacks. Olives and peanuts and a small mound of potato chips. The sun glinting on the oil of the olives made his mouth water and he realized he was starving.

The judge either didn't see them or chose not to. When they got to the back door he said, "I'll take my shoes off, don't want to track paint in."

The judge glanced up at the sound of his voice and then returned his attention to his paper without so much as acknowledging Eric's presence. He followed Tasmine into the house and up a flight of stairs. It was mostly bedrooms up here. Tasmine said, "She wants to redo a couple of the bedrooms for her grandchildren. We need to move a heavy dresser out of the way so I can see where the electric plugs are. That will affect the furniture placement and the kinds of pieces I will suggest."

"No problem." He followed her through a doorway and found himself in a nice sized bedroom with a dormer window. Mrs. Bailey sat on the bed contemplating a fan of fabric samples. This was clearly going to be a little girl's room since all the fabric included patterns in pink or purple.

An ornate, heavy oak dressing table complete with mirrors took up most of the opposite wall to the bed and it was this that had to be moved. He managed to shift the heavy beast far enough that Tasmine could see what was behind it.

"Thanks," she said.

"No problem." She'd mentioned a couple of things. "Anything else?"

"That rocker. If we move it out we'll get a better sense of the room, but I can do that."

"I got it." He picked up the old oak rocker and walked it out of the room and placed it in an alcove in the hallway where he figured it was out of the way. As he left the room, he heard Mrs. Bailey say, "He's so strong."

"He is," Tasmine agreed.

"Anything else?" he asked when he'd returned.

"No, that's good. Thanks, Eric."

He nodded.

As he was leaving Mrs. Bailey said, "I can't tell if these are bicycles or balloons. I've left my glasses downstairs in the kitchen. I'll just run down and get them."

He jogged down the stairs and back the way he'd come in. He was out the patio door and about to put on his shoes when he heard strange noises. He glanced up. The judge was jerking in his chair and getting red in the face. "Judge? Are you okay?"

Stupid thing to ask. The judge was a long way from okay

and, at Eric's words, put his hands around his throat in the classic 'I'm choking' signal.

He ran behind the older man and tried a sharp blow in between the shoulder blades.

No effect.

He rapidly reviewed what he remembered of the Heimlich maneuver. He'd studied it in first aid but he'd never used it. First time for everything. He knew the most important thing was not to panic. He got behind the judge, reached down, got his fisted hands above where he guessed the judge's navel to be, pushed into the fleshy paunch and then sharply up. The judge slumped over his arms and, not only had whatever was caught in the judge's throat not dislodged but Eric worried that the old guy was losing consciousness. "Stay with me, Judge."

CHAPTER 6

Feeling desperate now, and knowing he didn't have a lot of time, he pulled the judge right out of his chair and hauled him upright. He sucked in a breath, knowing he was going to need all his strength to dislodge whatever was stuck in the judge's throat.

He was about to try again when he heard a shriek from behind him.

"What are you doing?" He recognized Mrs. Bailey's voice but he didn't have time to stop and explain to her what was going on. He got his hands right onto the fleshy spot above the navel.

She screamed. "No! No! Leave him alone. Stop it! I'll call the police!" He felt a hard object smack him on the back and then the head and his back again. Meanwhile, she kept yelling. "Stop it, get away from him!" He tried to ignore her, and the pain of the blows raining down on him and focus on his task.

A new voice joined in the yelling. He heard Tasmine yell, "No. Mrs. Bailey. Stop! The Judge is choking. Eric's trying to save him."

He heard a struggle behind him and then the blows stopped.

He pulled his fisted hands right in under the judge's diaphragm and with all his strength yanked upwards.

He heard a sound like a pop and a gurgle and then a shiny green olive flew out of the judge's mouth and plopped to the ground at his feet. Eric half carried and half dragged the judge to the nearest patch of grass and laid him down. The old man dragged in a huge lungful of air and began to cough.

"What are you doing?" Mrs. Bailey yelled again, looking half hysterical.

He glanced over to where she was being held firmly. Tasmine had wrapped her arms around the woman to hold her in place and her small body was vibrating with anger and panic and confusion.

Tasmine repeated, "The judge was choking. Eric saved him." She held on one more second before releasing Mrs. Bailey.

The judge's wife ran forward and dropped to her knees at her husband's side. "Oh my dear, are you all right?"

The judge nodded. Slowly, he sat up. He looked up at Eric, "Thank you," he said in a raspy voice. "I'm obliged to you."

They sat side by side and Mrs. Bailey stroked her husband's back. "I didn't understand what was going on. I'm sorry, when I saw you with your arms around him I thought you were attacking him."

Eric was feeling a little shaky himself. Without permission he sank into one of the lounge chairs around the edge of the patio. The sight of those olives glistening in the sun no longer made him feel hungry.

"Mrs. Bailey," Tasmine said, "why don't I come back

tomorrow and we'll finish measuring for the furniture. If you have time, you can take a look at the fabric samples and let me know what you like."

"Yes, dear. If you don't mind, I think that would be best. I can't quite believe what just happened." She turned to her husband, "Should I call the doctor? Or an ambulance?"

He scowled at her. "No, I don't want to go to the hospital, and I don't want a doctor. I didn't choke to death, I don't have brain damage, and I don't want any fuss."

Eric stood. "I think I'll head off now, too." It was a little earlier than his usual quitting time but he didn't think anyone cared. "Good night, Judge Bailey. Night Mrs. Bailey." He walked over and picked up his shoes from the ground. He realized that Mrs. Bailey had used his own shoes as a weapon to hit him with. By the time he had his shoes back on, Tasmine had collected her bag from inside the kitchen, so they walked out together.

When they were out of earshot, Tasmine turned to him, "I've never seen that done before. It was amazing. He would be dead right now if it wasn't for you."

He nodded. "Probably."

They walked on a little more. He'd never saved anyone's life before. It was a powerful feeling.

"You know, you never know what things are for. Maybe there was a reason that you got in trouble with the judge and had to come back here and clean his pool. Maybe fate led you here, so you could save the judge's life."

"Be a lot easier if fate had stopped Mrs. Bailey from putting out olives today."

"Well, if you ask me, a man's life is worth a lot more than a painting."

The guilt he'd been carrying around lessened a notch. He looked down at her, "Thanks." Then he said, on impulse, "I'm hungry. Can I take you for dinner somewhere?"

"Oh. Sure. That would be nice."

He looked at her in her pretty summer dress and her heels and then down at himself. "I've got a clean shirt in the car and my gym bag, do you think the Baileys would let me shower in the pool house?"

"I think the Baileys would do anything for you right now," she replied, "but they've had a shock. Let's not bother them. You can shower at my place."

"You sure?"

"I'm sure."

He followed her to an apartment complex in Venice Beach. And when she drove her car into the underground parking he was able to find a spot on the street. He grabbed his gym bag out of the trunk and she came to the front door and let him in. They took the elevator up to the third floor and he followed her to her apartment. Once inside, he thought it was obvious that she was in the furniture or design business. Even though she hadn't known he was coming, the place looked professionally staged.

Now that he was here, she grew slightly nervous. "I only have one bathroom. You get to it through my bedroom."

He grinned at her. "Yeah? I get to see the room I've been dreaming about?"

She rolled her gaze. "Very funny. Towels are in the bathroom in the long cupboard."

He thanked her briefly, and headed to the only door that could possibly lead to her bedroom.

Everything about Tasmine's bedroom said that she was a

romantic. She had a big bed, the bedspread in a pale hue of purple that glowed with the sheen of silk. It was pretty obvious that her furniture came from that fancy furniture company she worked for. It was a lot nicer than what most people her age could afford. He was about to head for the bathroom when he stopped dead in his tracks.

"What the hell?" He must've said the words louder than he realized for Tasmine came running in.

"What's the matter?" Then she followed his gaze to where a very familiar bridal gown hung on her bedroom wall, mounted the way a big game hunter might mount a trophy.

Her hand flew to her cheek. "Oh my gosh, I forgot that was there. I'm so sorry. Is it painful for you?"

The last time he'd seen that gown, it had been hanging in Ashley's room, after his bride-to-be-had abandoned it, and him.

But, there had always been something kind of unreal about that whole wedding thing and, the way things had turned out, he thought he was going to be a whole lot better off. And he hoped Ashley would be too. "No. Not painful exactly. Doesn't bring back the greatest memories. But what's it doing here?"

She had that kind of fair skin that when she blushed, there was no denying her discomfort. "Ashley's aunt Millicent didn't want the dress, in fact, she wanted it gone, right off the property. Ashley's mom didn't want it either so she asked me to get rid of it. But it's such a beautiful gown. It really is a piece of art. So I thought I'd try hanging it on the wall."

He looked at the gown for a moment. He couldn't imagine going to bed and waking up with a great big dress hanging on his wall, but he was the first one to admit he didn't know much about art. Or fashion. He made a noncommittal sound, and continued on his way to the bathroom.

He stood gratefully under the pounding hot water, showering off the dirt and some of the fatigue of the day. Her towels were big, fluffy and purple. He pulled out the shaving kit he always kept in his gym bag, combed his hair, brushed his teeth, put on a clean pair of jeans and a clean shirt and felt like a new man.

When he walked into her main room, he discovered that while he was in the shower she'd changed her own clothes. She also wore jeans, and a blue shirt made of some kind of stretchy material with an alluring V in the front. She had taken her hair down so it hung in loose curls around her shoulders, exactly the way he liked it, but of course she didn't know that.

She had her laptop open and was drinking a glass of water. "I was just checking my email. Word's really got around about me. I've been asked to be a bridesmaid four more times this summer."

"That's a lot of weddings."

"I know. It's a nice side hustle for me. I get to wear pretty dresses and go to parties and I get paid for it."

Since he'd seen her at work on his own wedding, he knew how much effort went into her second job. He liked that she was such a go-getter. In fact, there was a lot he liked about Tasmine. "I wish somebody would pay me to go to weddings. I seem to have one every other weekend. I wonder if we're at any of the same ones?"

"I don't know." She pushed a couple keys on her laptop and up came a color-coded schedule on a calendar app. "Have a look." She stood. "Do you want water?"

"Sure." He scanned through the names and sure enough saw a familiar one. "You're doing Donovan and Kylie's wedding?"

"Yes, I am. I think probably it was Ashley who told Kylie about me."

"Well, now at least I'll have a reason to look forward to that one."

She handed him the water and didn't answer since she had no idea what to say.

He perused the calendar some more. "Stacey Cron is a friend of my sister's. They invited all of us. I was trying to get out of it, but if you're going, maybe I'll go too." He drank the water down while she closed her laptop and grabbed her bag.

He asked, " Do you have a favorite place around here?"

"There's a good Mexican place a couple of blocks from here."

"Perfect."

They walked the two blocks to the restaurant and sat outside on the patio. He ordered a beer, and she had a margarita and then he ordered the biggest combo platter on the menu while she ordered a taco salad.

She was good company, and he found her very easy to talk to. Plus, he didn't bother trying to impress her since she already knew he was a screw-up. Even though they were distant cousins who met somewhere in the family tree, he had a lot of distant cousins so their families had never been close. They'd spent some time together as kids, but he hadn't seen her for years. So, he asked all the usual first date questions. Not that this was a date, exactly, but being out for dinner with an attractive woman made him fall back on dating behavior.

He discovered that she enjoyed yoga, that she'd taken dance all through school and had been a cheerleader. If there was ever a woman born to shake pom-poms, it was Tasmine.

"So, you go to so many weddings, do you ever want to get married?"

She blinked at him and for some reason a slight blush stole into her cheeks. She glanced down at her salad and stabbed a chunk of lettuce. "Yes, of course I do." Then she glanced up and he saw that single dimple appear as she gave him her quirky smile. "And who could plan a more perfect wedding than me?" Then she said, "How about you? You've had a bad experience, do you think you'd tried again?"

"I think for guys it's different. I've always assumed I'll get married, in the same way I assume I'll get a job that involves wearing a suit and tie, and I'll join the same business club my father belongs to, but it's not like a big dream or anything."

She nodded. "Plus, I don't care what anyone says, women do have a biological clock ticking and men don't."

He looked slightly alarmed. "You have a biological ticking clock? Already? Aren't you kind of young?"

She laughed. "I'm twenty-six. Same age as you. But I don't want to be one of these women waiting until forty to have my first child. I love kids. I want to be young with them. I plan to have my first baby before thirty."

"Wow. That's quite a life plan you've got there. Got the guy picked out?"

"No. Some things, I leave to fate."

"Like the olives?"

She had a great laugh. "Something like that."

It was a nice walk back to her apartment and he felt an

urge to take her hand, but he didn't. This wasn't a real first date, she knew he'd only been un-engaged for a few weeks, and he didn't want to screw up a friendship that he was beginning to care about.

When they got back to her apartment, she hesitated outside and said, "Well, thanks a lot for dinner."

"You're welcome. I had fun. But I need to come up to your place. I left my gym bag in your bedroom."

She sent him a look, like, really?

"I didn't mean to. I forgot it was there."

"Well, you'd better come up and get it, then."

When they got to her place, he sprinted into her bedroom, grabbed his bag and returned, not wanting her to think he'd fake forgotten the bag. He never stooped to tricks like that. He'd never had to. When he came out of her bedroom, he noticed she'd flipped some lights on in her living room. She said, "I was just going to make some chamomile tea. Do you want some?"

He'd love to stay longer in her company, but he thought she was simply being polite. "I'd love to, but I've got to drive home and then I have to be at work at seven in the morning."

"Right, I forgot you still lived at home." She made him sound like one of those failure-to-launch slackers, which he supposed he was. He had the money from his trust fund if he wanted to go get an apartment, but he'd never had any reason to leave. Everything was taken care of at home; he liked his parents, had a wing of the house pretty much to himself and Millie to pack his lunches. But, Tasmine's comment made him think that if he was more independent she would find him more interesting. It was something to think about.

She rose to see him out. "That was amazing what you did

today. I need to refresh my CPR and my first aid. I don't think I can remember how to do the Heimlich maneuver."

"I didn't think I remembered, either. But it's amazing how that stuff comes back to you in an emergency." Then he said, "Come here. I'll show you."

CHAPTER 7

*S*he walked closer. He explained how to make the fist with her thumb side toward the victim's body and then gently nudged her up against him. He wrapped his arms around her and brought his fisted hands gently under ribs. "You see, what you have to do is press in and up so you force the air from the diaphragm to dislodge whatever's caught in the person's throat. With Judge Bailey, I don't think I was forceful enough at first so it took a few tries.

He pressed ever so gently against her, giving her the feel of pressure against her diaphragm.

Unlike the judge, Tasmine had the abs of an athlete. Where she was pressed against him, he felt the warmth of her back against his front as a current of awareness flowed between them. When he looked down over her shoulder in the direction of his fisted hands he could see down the alluring V of her top. She had nice curves on her, that was for sure.

They stayed like that for quite a few seconds longer than was necessary for his demonstration and then he stepped back and said, "Why don't you try it on me?"

She turned around so she was facing him. "Me? Try it on you? Don't you have to be a lot bigger than the person?"

"I don't know. Probably, if I was choking, I'd be sitting down. Let's try it." He was curious to know whether it would work or not. He was as much at risk of choking as anybody else. He didn't want to think that he was doomed to die just because most people in the world were smaller than him. He settled himself in one of the chairs at the fancy bistro set and she came up behind him. He put his hands to his throat in the classic I'm choking gesture, similar to what the judge had done earlier.

She bent down, clasping her hands together into a fist as he'd showed her and then scooping her arms around him and aiming for the same spot on his belly, in between the ribs and the navel. In order to make it easier for her he leaned forward so that when she scooped in she got the right spot. She put her all into it and the result was that he felt like his lungs were being squeezed, and he gave an *oof* that he was pretty sure would send a stray olive flying. "Okay, I think you got it." He put his hands over hers. "Nice job."

Her hair hung down and a curl brushed his shoulder. He could smell something flowery that she used on her hair, and underneath that, her own scent, as individual as DNA. He thought he could sit here and breathe her in all day.

"Thanks. It's a good thing to know. I should really get my CPR and first aid updated. You never know when someone's going to need your help." He stood up, reminding himself that she had not invited him up to her apartment. He had come up to pick up his bag, and he did not want her to think he was a man she couldn't trust.

He headed back towards the door where'd he dropped his

bag earlier and picked it up. "Thanks again for coming out with me. Maybe we can do it again sometime?"

She came forward so she was standing within a foot of him. "I'd like that."

"Okay, then."

He didn't open the door. She didn't open it for him. He felt the possibility of a kiss floating in the air. He didn't want to blow this relationship. If she only wanted to be his friend, he didn't want to mess that up. He was beginning to realize that he needed to get himself some new friends. His old buddies were great for a laugh, but he was getting a feeling, like an itch under his skin, that he was stuck in some bad patterns and that it was time to change.

Ashley had done that. As much as the humiliation of the wedding day still hurt, Ash and he had not been good for each other. She'd found Ben, and then suddenly she was learning to drive and helping an A list screenwriter with his screenplays. She'd moved on, and he hadn't.

Tasmine, he realized, had a lot of qualities he admired. She was smart, independent, ambitious, and hardworking. In his life so far, he had been exactly none of those things. Well, except smart, but how would anyone ever know that? He'd hidden it so well.

Tasmine was also sexy as hell. He wanted to pull her against him and kiss the breath out of her, and see if he could talk his way into that big beautiful bed of hers. But, he was pretty sure that wasn't going to happen. He could give her a quick hug, the kind of thing that he did with his female friends when there was nothing between them. But that seemed so cold.

So, figuring he had nothing to lose, he went for something

in the middle. He leaned in and, if she turned her face he would've kissed her cheek, but she didn't so he pressed his mouth briefly to hers. It was the briefest touch of lips and yet he felt warmth and softness and, unless he was completely crazy, he felt a slight tremor run through her that fired his blood.

It took all his willpower to pull away. "Will I see you tomorrow?"

She nodded. "I'll finish up measuring the bedrooms that Mrs. Bailey wants to decorate."

"Well, you'll know where to find me."

TASMINE CHECKED in with her office first thing the next morning. She took care of a few emails, checked on a ship-ment that had been delayed, and then headed for the Bailey's estate. She felt stupidly jumpy at the notion of seeing Eric again. What was the matter with her? He barely even knew she existed. Had been engaged to someone else until she'd left him at the altar. He'd pretty much made it clear he only wanted to be friends with Tasmine. Which was good for her. She couldn't afford to get sidetracked from her life plan.

She was proud of how far she'd come in her twenty-six years on earth. Unlike Eric, she had worked for everything she had and now possessed a good degree, a job she enjoyed, and a part-time bridesmaid gig that was building her savings nicely. But she still had a long way to go.

An overgrown juvenile delinquent like Eric was not part of her plan. She shouldn't feel jumpy at the idea of seeing him.

It was that kiss. So brief that it could barely even be called a kiss, the swiftest pressing together of lips. And yet, she had felt something. Something she hadn't felt in her previous relationships. She could not even imagine what he could do to her if he put some effort into it. She had to remind herself to be on guard. She was convenient for Eric, the perfect rebound love affair after Ashley. But she was not interested in being anyone's rebound. She was looking for the real thing. Even if Eric made her toes curl, he was not for her.

But, when she got to the Baileys' place, she couldn't stop herself from first going to see Eric.

His back was to her when she came to the edge of the pool. He was giving it a new layer of paint, doing a careful, thorough job. He had his earbuds in his ears so he hadn't heard her approach. She took a moment to enjoy looking at him. Tall, broad-shouldered, and muscular. He was clearly an athletic guy, but these weeks he'd spent at hard physical labor had toughened him up. As he painted she could see the movement of muscles in his back even under his shirt, and his exposed arms were as cut as a professional athlete's. She could have watched him paint all day. His skin was bronzed, kissed by the sun, and the way he slapped paint on a pool bed was poetry in motion.

She didn't move, or call out, but suddenly he stopped painting and, as though aware of her presence, turned slowly to face her. When their gazes connected she felt the sucker punch of lust.

She waved, trying to give the impression that she had only arrived that second, not that she had been standing there drooling over his gorgeous body for the last couple of minutes. He put down the paintbrush and pulled out his earbuds. "Morning," he said, giving her his slow, easy smile.

He was too much of a charmer. She could almost imagine that he was attracted to her as she was to him.

"What are you listening to?" she asked, wondering if they shared any taste in music and suspecting they probably didn't.

"Stephen Hawking," he said.

She laughed. Always with the jokes. "Okay, don't tell me. It's probably one of those awful rap songs with misogynistic lyrics."

He merely shrugged his powerful shoulders. "You back on decorating duty?"

"Yes. I'm headed for the main house. Thought I'd check and see if you needed anything." Really? What was she, his mother?

"Millie packed me enough lunch to feed most of California. If you get finished and feel like a sandwich and her most excellent apple cake come back and join me."

"Thanks." Even though she knew his only other option other than eating with her was to lunch by himself, she still felt excited by his casual offer, as though he'd invited her to the prom.

When she went to the main house, Mrs. Bailey seemed genuinely pleased to see her. "Oh my dear, do come in. Do you have time for cup of coffee before we start?"

Usually, Tasmine tried to keep her clients focused on the work. But she liked Mrs. Bailey, and besides, she felt that her client needed to talk. She could imagine that having her husband almost choke to death yesterday had shaken her up.

"Sure. How's the judge feeling today?"

"He's fine. The only lasting injury was to his pride."

Maria served them coffee in a pretty room that overlooked the rose garden. She supposed it would be a morning room.

The furniture was overstuffed chintz and family portraits cluttered every surface. Maria brought the coffee on a silver tray that gleamed from a recent polishing. The cups, the coffee pot, and the creamer and sugar bowl were made of the most exquisite china, which she thought might be Sevres. A plate with two kinds of cookies also sat on the tray. She wondered what it would be like to be this rich and was fairly certain she'd never know.

"Thank you, Maria." Mrs. Bailey poured the coffee herself and handed it to Tasmine, inviting her to help herself to cream and sugar. Then she offered her the plate of cookies. "These are the cook's own recipe. They are the most delicious ginger cookies. She protects the recipe fiercely and won't share it with anyone. There's also shortbread if you prefer."

"Thank you," Tasmine said, choosing one of Cook's famous ginger cookies. She bit into the crunchy, richly spiced treat and agreed that they were indeed delicious.

Tasmine waited and soon Mrs. Bailey said, "First, I wanted to thank you for keeping a clear head yesterday. I don't know what came over me. I came down to get my glasses and I saw what I thought was a man attacking my husband. Even when I realized it was Eric, I had this terrible impression he was trying to hurt my husband." She raised her faded blue eyes to Tasmine's and she could see the stricken look in them. "If I had succeeded in stopping Eric, my husband might have died."

"Mrs. Bailey, you acted on instinct. It was easier for me because I could clearly see what was happening. Don't be too hard on yourself. Everything worked out fine."

The old woman nodded. "The judge and I had a long talk last night." She shook her head. "It's funny how one moment can change everything. I could have lost my husband if it weren't for Eric's quick action and bravery. What is one painting compared to my husband's life? I could bear to lose every piece of artwork in this house, and the house itself, before I could bear to lose my husband."

"I know." She couldn't be married to Judge Bailey for five minutes without wanting to smack him, but she could see the deep love that existed between these two.

"I suggested to the judge that perhaps we should tell Eric that due to his prompt and heroic behavior yesterday, we consider his debt to us to be erased. And do you know what Ernest said to me?"

Tasmine shook her head. She somehow doubted that Judge Bailey was quite as forgiving as his wife.

"He said I should discuss the matter with you." She smiled her sweet smile. "The judge thinks very highly of your judgment, you know. Well, we both do. And you seem to understand Eric so well. What would you advise us?"

Tasmine sipped her coffee to give her a moment to absorb the fact that they were considering letting Eric off completely from his chores. She also had to take in the fact that two people of such intelligence and stature in the world would turn to her for advice. She set her coffee cup down, and gazed out the window for a moment. She didn't want to blurt anything out, but to give the best advice she was capable of.

It was surprisingly easy to find the right answer, or what seemed to her to be the right answer. "You know, ever since Eric started working here, he's been changing. I don't know if he even realizes it himself. But he's taking pride in that job. It's the worst job I can even imagine, but I've been checking up on him. He doesn't slack off when he thinks no one's watching and he's doing a good job. I feel like he's taking responsibility for his actions for the first time and it's good for him. Honestly, I think you should keep him working." Then she grinned at the older woman. "But, maybe when he finishes the pool you could find him some jobs that are less disgusting."

"I see what you are saying. I do want to express my gratitude to him, though. And so does the judge."

"Maybe the best way to do that is to do what you did with me. Offer him a cup of coffee once in a while or maybe an iced tea at the end of his workday. I think there is more to Eric than any of us realized. Let's let him find it."

"Well, if you're sure."

"Of course I'm not sure. I could be completely wrong. But, in my heart, this feels right."

"It's funny, isn't it? The twists and turns that fate takes in one's life. If I hadn't gone to Paris that summer, I never would have fallen in love with painting the way I have. Or discovered artists who have gone on to become famous, partly, I like to think, through my influence. And, perhaps, if Eric hadn't done that foolish, foolish thing, and you hadn't suggested that his punishment take the form of hard work on our property, then my husband might have choked to death yesterday."

It was strange that Mrs. Bailey was voicing so much of what she herself had said yesterday. "Fate is a strange and mysterious force," she agreed.

"Well, I'd better stop wasting your time. I think I've chosen the fabrics I'd like for both of the bedrooms. I'm very excited to do these rooms over especially for my grandchildren. In fact, I hope you'll get to meet them."

"I hope so too."

They didn't talk about Eric or yesterday's incident any more after that. They went upstairs and between websites and catalogs of the various products her company represented, they were able to get everything ordered from the curtains to the furniture and even some accessories that were kid-friendly.

When they were done, she was almost as excited as Mrs. Bailey. She glanced at her watch and saw that it was after noon.

Mrs. Bailey said, "Maria serves lunch at twelve-thirty. The judge should be back by then. Would you care to join us?"

Wow. She doubted many furniture suppliers would be asked to lunch. Unlike Grace Van Hoffendam, who had always made sure to remind Tasmine that she was hired help, Mrs. Bailey and the judge seemed like they appreciated people for their personal qualities rather than their net worth. She thought they were much nicer people.

"Thank you. But I already agreed to eat lunch with Eric. Their housekeeper packs him these massive lunches."

"Well, I am very glad he has you for a friend."

Tasmine nodded and began gathering her things. And wasn't that great, that even Mrs. Bailey saw her and Eric as nothing more than friends. Why hadn't he patted her on the back last night, or given her a quick hug like people do when they're friends? Even though the kiss was the shortest kiss in the history of kissing, she couldn't stop thinking about it.

CHAPTER 8

A stronger woman would skip out on lunch, but she wasn't that strong. She wanted to see Eric. And, strangely, she didn't want to let him down.

When she got back to the pool area, he was still hard at work. This time, instead of stopping to stare at him longingly, she walked around the pool so that she was facing him, leaned down and waved her arms.

He waved back, then put down his tools, took out his earbuds, and climbed out of the pool. "I hope you're hungry."

"For one of Millie's sandwiches? Always."

He set his iPod down on the patio table and said, "I'll go wash up and get lunch."

"Okay." She settled herself at the table and tipped her head back, enjoying being outside on such a beautiful day. She picked up the iPod, wondering what he really had been listening to, placed the earbuds in her own ears and pressed play. To her shock, she couldn't hear any offensive rap music, or music of any kind. A man's voice was explaining, in a British accent, something about time.

When Eric returned with the bag containing their lunch, she said, "You really were listening to Stephen Hawking's book."

"I was."

"Wow. You are full of surprises."

He passed her a package of sandwiches, and when their gazes connected there was a certain disturbing gleam in his eye. "Oh, you have no idea."

Why did he have to do this? Now he was flirting with her. But it was like that kiss last night, brief and teasing and she could imagine it didn't mean anything if she wanted to. But what if she wanted it to mean something?

As they munched their sandwiches and drank the cooled cans of soda, she said, "Millie can make me lunch anytime."

He leaned back. "Do you have a wedding this Saturday?"

She shook her head. "I have a blissful, wedding-free weekend."

"I'm thinking about going for a hike on Saturday. Up to Sandstone Peak in the Santa Monica Mountains. Would you like to come? Millie will pack lunch."

She stared at him. "After you've put in five days of hard, physical labor, you want to spend your free time hiking? I would've thought you'd spend it lounging around."

He shook his head. "I'm not big on lounging. Too much energy. I like to stay active. Preferably outdoors."

Her plans for the weekend had included laundry, getting her hair cut, maybe catching up with some girlfriends and hitting the gym. She thought that going hiking with Eric would be a lot more fun than all those other things put together. Plus, it could replace her gym workout. So she nodded. "Thanks. I'd like that."

"Cool. I'll pick you up at nine?"

"Perfect."

"And remember, I'm bringing lunch."

"Can I put in a special request for more of this apple cake?"

"On it."

Their conversation was as easy and casual as ever, but she felt that niggle of irritation that would not leave her. What did going hiking mean? If he'd asked her to dinner, or a movie, that implied it was romantic. But hiking? That was the sort of activity that you did with your buddies. Was she his buddy?

Even though Eric had assured her that he would bring lunch for their hike, Tasmine still made sure to pack some emergency food supplies as well as a bladder of water and her first aid kit. It was another gorgeous, sunny day. She hesitated over her choice of hats. There was the pink ball cap, and then there was the hiking hat made of sun-protective fabric. If this was a date, she knew she'd be strongly tempted to wear the cute ball cap. But she wasn't going to risk premature aging and sunburn for a guy who seemed to view her as a gal pal.

She determined to put aside all questions of what the relationship was and what she wanted it to be, and simply enjoy the day.

Eric arrived right on time, which impressed her. He wore hiking shorts with multiple pockets, a decent and well-worn pair of boots, and a pack large enough that she suspected there would be no need of her emergency food supplies. "It looks like Millie outdid herself."

"Oh yeah, she always thinks we'll starve to death if she doesn't feed us all day long." He said the words with affection, though, and she could see that the cook was an important person in his life.

"Did you do anything exciting last night?" Since he had arrived on time, she suspected he had not partied all night.

He glanced over at her, and then back up the road. "Are you joking? I barely get through dinner and then I crash for the night. The only social thing I've done since I started at the Gulag is dinner with you the other night."

Immediately, her neurotic brain began to sift through the meaning of his words. Okay, he considered their dinner social, did that mean a date? Or not?

"And today."

He sounded a little sorry for himself so she reminded him that her life wasn't all sunshine and roses either. "Most of my social life revolves around weddings, which, for me, is a business."

"So getting out in the mountains today is a big deal for you, too."

"It sure is."

"Do you get sick of weddings?"

It was funny how many people asked her that question. She tried to answer honestly. "You know, I never do. There is something magical about a wedding, about seeing two people who learned to love each other in spite of their imperfections and who have made this amazing commitment to spend the rest of their lives together. We don't have a lot of big ceremonies in our culture. I think celebrating a wedding, putting on that special gown, announcing in front of God and your friends and family that you are committing to this other person, is fantastic." She quickly reviewed the past few weddings, and added, "I'm not saying it's always perfect. Brides can get a little difficult and emotional when the big day approaches, and it can be stressful for me, because little things always go wrong and it's up to me to fix them, but the actual ceremony? When they share that first kiss as man and wife? I pretty much always shed a tear at that moment."

"Wow. You really are romantic."

"You say that like it's a bad thing."

"No. I thought you'd be all cynical and down on weddings, because you must see the people you work with at their worst."

"Oh, I do. But then, I also get to see them at their best. They're human, and if they believe enough, and love each other enough, I think it will work."

His fingers tapped on the steering wheel and she realized that she had been talking without realizing that his wedding hadn't gone remotely as planned. He said, "Well, obviously that was the problem with me and Ashley. We did not love each other enough. I've been thinking about what you said, about how selfish it was to use her like that. Honestly, I never thought it through. I didn't mean to hurt her. She's a great girl. I thought, I have to get married anyway, a lot of our friends are doing it, and it would help me out of a jam, so why not?"

He turned to glance at her once more, "But you made me see how wrong we were. I wish I could make it up to her."

She really liked that he was willing to own his mistakes. She liked even more that he had listened to her and taken her words to heart. However, she tried to be an honest woman, and she suspected he was beating himself up needlessly. "I think it's great that you're trying to see this from Ashley's point of view. But, honestly? Would she and Ben have realized how they felt about each other if she hadn't been engaged? I mean, talk about figuring it out at the last minute."

Suddenly he laughed. "I will never forget your face, when I showed up right before the wedding. And then I walked into that room and I saw the window wide open and I knew she'd run."

"You looked sick."

"I was terrified that I'd be going to jail. But deep down, I think I felt a little relieved."

"You probably weren't ready to get married."

There was a pause, then he said, "I definitely wasn't ready to marry Ashley."

THEY GOT to the trailhead and unloaded. She put on her butt-ugly hat and he shoved a ball cap over his head. They hefted their packs and headed for the trail.

It was so nice to be out in the mountains and the fresh air, away from the city, her weekend routines, and weddings. To spend a Saturday in hiking boots instead of high heels, her hair shoved under a hat instead of styled by a professional, and to wear no more makeup than a swish of lip gloss felt great.

They hiked at an easy pace, neither trying to impress the other. They disturbed a snake sunning itself on the trail, which slid away instantly. As they climbed, she began to get views of the ocean and the nearby islands. "It is so beautiful here," she said.

"God's country," he agreed.

When they reached the peak, he found them a flat spot with a view and they settled, with their backs against a couple of large rocks, to eat their lunch.

They munched Millie's amazing sandwiches and ate the apple cake. She pulled out a slab of chocolate.

She turned to him. "Why do you hide how smart you are?"

He looked uncomfortable. "Who says I'm smart?"

"I do."

She thought for a moment that he wasn't going to answer; she could almost see him gearing up to make a joke. And then, as though he realized that she was on to him, he dropped the teasing act and said, "Sometimes it's easier to be the kid nobody expects anything from."

She knew he was telling the truth, but she was genuinely puzzled. "But your family seems so . . ." She didn't quite know how to put this without sounding offensive. "So success oriented."

"Yeah, I know. But I'm the youngest. My brother was always the one that had all the expectations piled on him. And, it was like he already had the Smart Spot, my sister already had the Girl Spot, that kind of left the Clown Spot open."

"The Clown Spot?"

"I know it sounds crazy. But when I was growing up, my brother would bring home his excellent report cards and my folks pretty much piled on the expectations. Of course, I was younger. If I tried to say anything, he just shut me down and made me look stupid. And, I don't know, I always had a gift for making people laugh. My mom used to call me her little clown. After a while, I figured out that if I started acting stupid everyone was happy. Plus, it was a lot easier on me. My folks pressured him pretty hard. Now, he's driven, he's successful, but it's like his whole life is a report card, you know what I mean?"

"Sort of. I don't have any personal experience with that, because my folks only wanted us to find a decent career, maybe one day buy a house, hopefully find a partner, you know, live a reasonably happy life."

"I think the Van Hoffendams still have that mentality that their sons and daughters are supposed to lead society and excel in business. I don't think a reasonably happy life would be very high on their agenda."

"So, by being happy and not trying very hard you were a complete rebel."

"I guess."

"But you are smart." She'd met his brother, who was supposed to be one of the groomsmen at Eric's wedding. Tom was a pompous man, older than his years, who, if he had any sense of humor at all, kept it well hidden. She hadn't talked to Tom very much, but from what she overheard, he used big words when small ones would be more effective. "In fact, I suspect you have a much higher IQ than your brother does."

"Probably."

He put a casual arm around her and pulled her close. Even though he didn't say anything, she could see him smiling. She thought that he was happy to have someone from whom he did not have to hide his intelligence. He tilted his head so he was looking at her. "Are you going to keep my secrets?"

There was an unmistakable gleam in his eyes. This was not the way a man looked at his hiking buddy but the way a man looks at a woman when he's thinking about kissing her. She felt a shiver of attraction as soft as a light breeze skip across her skin. She was caught in his gaze, and when he shifted so that his mouth was an inch away from hers, in perfect kissing distance, she didn't pull away or do anything but feel her lips open in anticipation. He didn't lunge at her right away, he looked as though he were anticipating the moment before the kiss.

She felt the delicious tension building in her belly, watched in fascination as his mouth grew slowly closer, and then she closed her eyes, and savored the moment his lips touched hers. His body brushed against her, soft and tantalizing, and he slowly deepened the kiss. Her heart began to pound and she felt lightheaded. She couldn't stop herself from putting her arms around him and pulling him even closer. She tasted the salt of their workout. She felt how solid his body was, tough with muscle, and when he trailed his fingertips across her collarbone, she felt the calluses of a man who works with his hands.

She could not stop the moan of pleasure, as he toyed with her mouth, teasing a response out of her, though, in fact, no teasing was necessary. She would give him anything in this moment. She suspected from the masterful way he handled her that he knew it, too.

She had no idea what might have happened next if they hadn't heard the unmistakable sound of more hikers approaching the summit. He didn't scramble off her, he simply moved slowly away from her and settled back against his rock. By the time the hikers had arrived, he was packing up the last of their lunch.

She tried to act equally cool, sitting up slowly and reaching for her water bottle as though a few sips of water could cool the burning in her system.

It was a family who arrived with them on top of the mountain. "Hi," the dad said. He was followed by his wife, presumably, and two young teenagers both looking as though they'd rather still be in bed.

"Hi," Eric said. "Nice day."

"Sure is."

He rose and hoisted the pack onto his back, and she stood up and put on her own much smaller pack. They said goodbye to the family and started back down the path. Where they'd chatted so easily on the way up, well, except for the parts where she couldn't talk because she was breathing so hard from exertion, on the way down she felt shy. Once more, she had no idea what that kiss had meant. He didn't seem in any hurry to enlighten her. He wasn't very chatty either, though, and she wondered whether he was regretting taking advantage of that moment.

She decided the best thing to do was to put it out of her mind, and not obsess in some neurotic fashion all the way down the hill. So, she put on the voice she used with her customers when she needed to coax them into a decision. "You will never believe what color Stacey Cron chose for our bridesmaid dresses."

"Red?"

"Worse. So much worse. The color is called lemon chiffon. I swear, it's exactly the same color as dog pee in snow. And with my hair color? I can't even tell you how bad I look in my bridesmaid dress."

"You'll look great," he assured her.

And what on earth had possessed her to tell him the color looked like dog pee on snow? She did not want him looking at her and thinking about canine urine. She only blurted out stupid things like this when she was nervous. And it annoyed her that he made her nervous. What was he thinking, kissing her and leaving no clue as to what he meant by it? The first time, his kiss had been about as passionate as a hug. Her reaction had been far from casual. Now, today, he'd really heated things up, and then acted like nothing happened. No, worse, he'd grown quiet, like he might be regretting the impulse.

She really needed to stop making herself crazy over this guy. Except, she saw him in a way no one else did. The fact that he'd not made a joke or pushed her away when she'd challenged him on his obvious intelligence had her feeling like she had a kind of intimacy with him that he didn't share with everybody. But what did she really know about Eric Van Hoffendam? Well, most of what she knew about him wasn't actually that great. So why did she continue in this stubborn belief that she was the only one who could see the amazing person he could become if he'd only apply himself?

They continued to chat on impersonal subjects on the way down. The strange thing was, it was a lot easier to talk going down, when they were breathing normally, and yet, they seemed to have less to talk about. She felt the kiss between them like a huge stop sign waving in front of her face. She didn't want to act in a way that would suggest to him how much that kiss had meant to her. It was easier to act as though it hadn't happened at all.

When they got to the bottom of the path and returned to the car, he said, "Thanks for coming today. I really needed to get out and away from the city. It was great to have the company."

"It was fun, thanks for inviting me. And thank Millie for the sandwiches."

He drove them back to her place. She'd kept the evening free in case he wanted to do dinner or stop for a beer on the way home, but he didn't suggest anything. She felt fluttery when he pulled up in front of her place. Did she invite him up? It was a Saturday afternoon, and they both needed to shower, but if she asked him up to her place he was going to think she wanted sex. If he invited her for dinner, or to the beach, or back to his place for a dip in the pool, of course she'd say yes. If he even suggested he wanted to see more of her, then she could invite him up to her place without seeming like she was sex-starved and desperate. But, after looking at her for a moment, almost as though waiting for something, he said, "Hey, thanks again for today. " He got out and retrieved her pack for her.

She forced a smile. "I really had a great time."

He leaned in and gave her a swift kiss. "See you on Monday."

"Yeah, see you."

CHAPTER 9

*E*ric pulled away, cursing himself for a fool. What was the matter with him? Why did he keep hitting on Tasmine?

She'd been acting strange ever since that kiss. He knew he shouldn't have done it, but when she snuggled up against him, with her head on his chest, he had the feeling that she saw him, saw through his usual bluster and his class clown persona, to the brain he usually either tried to hide, or used to think up increasingly stupid pranks. He had felt a moment of intimate connection. He could not have prevented himself kissing her any more than he could've prevented those hikers from showing up right when things were getting interesting.

He'd hoped against hope that she would invite him up for a cold drink of water, suggest a beer, anything that would give him hope that she liked him. But she hadn't. Instead, he'd felt her growing more distant. He'd made it obvious from that kiss that he had a crush on the woman they jokingly referred to as his parole officer. In return, she had made it pretty clear that she wasn't interested.

And yet, the way she'd responded had blown his mind. He felt as though he were losing his edge, losing the cheerful confidence he'd always had around women. Between Ashley dumping his ass and Tasmine saving it from jail, he'd really started to question a lot of his assumptions about himself and women. If he drove Tasmine away, he didn't think he could handle it. He needed her in his life, even if only as a friend.

He made a vow to himself to stop pushing himself at her, at least until she gave some definite sign that she was interested. Sure, she hadn't exactly pushed them away today, and the way her body had responded against his had him feeling like he needed to hike up another mountain just to get rid of this excess energy.

Maybe he'd offer to drive her to the Cron wedding they were both attending. Of course, she probably had to be there hours before he did, but at least he'd get to spend time with her and he'd be able to drive her home at the end of the party. It was the kind of move that if she wanted only friendship, she could accept his friendship, a guy doing her a favor. And if she wanted to give him any sign at all that she was interested in him he'd be all over it.

HE HAD WONDERED if the Baileys might go easier on him now that he'd saved the judge from death by choking. But, apart from the judge thanking him right after it happened, no one had said anything.

However, things did start to change. Once he'd finished painting the pool, José took over and checked all the hoses and filters before having it filled with fresh water.

He got put on regular gardening detail. He found himself hauling paving stones, mowing grass and weeding. His podcasts and audiobooks were more and more related to gardening, landscaping, and drought-resistant gardening in particular.

He could see how much water was getting sucked up by the traditional plants and, even worse, by the lawns, and thought it was not only unsustainable, but that more native and drought resistant plants would look better.

He broached the idea with José, who, after his usual stream of Spanish abuse that made the other gardeners laugh, said, "You want to make more work for yourself? Go ahead, my friend. Talk to the judge."

So, he did. And to Mrs. Bailey. He'd picked one area, where there was little shade and no shelter from the elements and where the flowers were losing a battle against the climate. He drew up a plan at night, sketched in plants he'd read about and presented the idea to the Baileys when they were finishing their day out on the patio. He was happy to see the snacks did not include olives.

"Can I talk to you a minute?" he asked them.

"Certainly," the judge said.

"Sit down," Mrs. Bailey said. "Would you like a drink?"

He couldn't believe he was being treated like a guest instead of a slave. "Some water would be great."

She got up herself and fetched sparkling water, which she served in a crystal glass with ice and a slice of lemon.

He felt a little nervous coming to them with ideas on changing landscaping they'd probably lived with forever, but he could see in his head how much better the property could look. He pulled from his back pocket the diagram he'd made, explained why he was suggesting various plants. "The *Calandrinia*, that's the pink flowering one, will work really well with the succulents. I'd like to see yarrow and lavender, myrtle and drought-tolerant grasses. You'll not only save water and fertilizer but a lot of these attract birds and butterflies."

"Even bees," Mrs. Bailey said, studying his sketch. "I like the color spectrum, and you've got an interesting array of shapes."

She was an art lover, of course she understood that a garden was a kind of canvas. "Exactly. And I'm trying to work out a plan with plants that bloom at different times of year so there's always color."

"You should talk to José," the judge said.

"I did. He said to talk to you."

The judge tapped his fingers on the glass tabletop. "He'll make you do all the work, you know that, right?"

"That's what I'm here for."

"Martha?"

"I think it's a wonderful idea," she said. "I've been thinking for a while now that we should be more eco friendly."

"Draw up your list of supplies and give it to José. I'll talk to him and let him know you've got my permission."

He was excited to try out his ideas. Grateful the Baileys hadn't laughed at him and tossed his ideas back. There was so much potential to be more environmentally sustainable on the Baileys' property. Where the head gardener had started out thinking he was a lazy good-for-nothing, he thought his animosity now had more to do with seeing him as competition. Which was an improvement of sorts.

Even one small change was a beginning.

TASMINE HAD TOLD him that her dress looked the color of dog pee on snow. But when he picked her up the morning of the Cron wedding, to drop her off at the downtown hotel where the wedding would take place later that day, he thought she looked as cool and crisp as a newly sliced lemon. There was something so fresh about her, her hair was in some kind of an updo, and she already had her makeup done for the wedding. He loved her long, slender legs and the way those legs looked in a pair of lemon-colored high heels. She wheeled a weekend-sized traveling case behind her, and he already knew that it contained all sorts of emergency supplies, extra makeup, and probably a few extra blowup bridesmaids in case somebody got sick and didn't turn up. She was the most organized woman he'd ever known.

"This is so nice of you," she said.

"I had to go downtown anyway," he lied. In fact, he planned to spend a few hours at his club working out, maybe enjoy a steam room and a massage, and spend the day more like the Eric Van Hoffendam he used to be than the Eric who was a mistrusted garden slave. José still treated him like he was lower than the dirt they tilled.

He didn't see Tasmine again until the wedding. When she walked up the aisle he watched her all the way. At one point, as though she felt his gaze on her, she turned her head and their gazes connected. She might look cool and crisp on the outside but after their kiss, he knew how hot she burned. As though she could read his thoughts, her eyes widened slightly and then she was past him, heading for the front of the church.

At the reception, Tasmine was seated at the head table, of course, while he was at a table with friends he hadn't seen for months given his long hours in the Gulag.

Slade and Toad were there, Melissa and Douglass, who were going to have about six kids before they even got married if they didn't leave each other alone, and Kylie and Donovan who were gearing up for their own wedding in a few weeks. A couple of unattached women were also at their table.

One of them, whose name was Kelly something, leaned close to him and said, "You are so tanned. I bet you're a surfer."

"Would be if I had time."

"Because you're too busy sailing? I love sailing. If you ever want to go sometime–"

Kelly was dark-haired, vivacious and in a different time he'd have been very interested in what she was offering. But right now he wished it was Tasmine sitting beside him. He interrupted her to say, "I'm a working stiff."

"A working stiff?"

"Yep. I work outside, gardening mostly."

"Oh," she sounded very disappointed.

Toad piped up. "Nobody's seen you, Hoff. It's like you fell off the planet."

Toad knew exactly where he was working, and why, but he supposed his old gang were having trouble accepting that he couldn't work crazy long hours breaking his back under the hot sun and also hang out and party all night.

He'd looked forward to seeing them all tonight but strangely he felt like they were still talking about the same things, still doing the same things, and he'd somehow moved on.

Kelly transferred her interest to Slade, Douglas and Melissa—who'd spent all their time touching and stroking each other—left early, Kylie and Donovan argued about their wedding cake choice, and he excused himself to mingle.

He managed to get a dance with Tasmine, a chance to hold her against him and imagine they were an item. "Having a good time?" she asked.

"I am now."

"Your table looks like fun."

"It was until Kylie and Donovan started arguing about wedding cakes. Fruitcake or chocolate. They wanted every-one's opinion."

"What did you say?"

"Doesn't matter. No one ever eats wedding cake anyway."

She laughed and he felt happier just being near her.

"When can you get away?"

"Right after the bride throws the bouquet."

"You aiming to catch it?"

She made a *pfft* sound. "If I catch the bouquet I might have to organize another wedding."

An hour later, it was Kelly who had caught the bouquet, and Tasmine was free to go.

He drove her home with care, knowing how many crazies were out on a summer Saturday. He'd made sure to drink nothing more serious than soda water knowing he'd be driving. Besides, there was something he really needed to talk to her about.

CHAPTER 10

*I*t was so nice having Eric drive her home. She could imagine that they were more than friends. That, like Melissa and Douglas, they left the second they could so they could rush home and get naked.

"I had an interesting conversation with the judge yesterday," Eric said, immediately derailing her train of thought.

"Really?"

"Yes. He's taken to hanging out with me for a little bit now and then. He's interested in the plants I'm choosing and why. Did you know that man has a sense of humor?"

She was jolted by surprise. "Are we talking about the same judge?"

"I know, right? Anyway, we were joking about olives."

"You were joking about olives with the man who nearly choked to death on one?"

"You kind of had to be there."

"Okay."

"We started by talking about varieties of olive trees that

grow best in this climate and then one thing led to another and we were talking about death by olive." She couldn't imagine the judge and Eric yukking it up over a near death experience and was still trying to process the strange notion when he shocked her to her core.

"Anyway, since he was in such a good mood, I said, 'Maybe, since I saved your life, you might let me out of the Gulag.'"

"You did not seriously use the word Gulag?" She felt like her upper ribs were squeezing in so her breath wasn't coming into her lungs as easily as it normally did.

"I absolutely did."

She shifted, trying to loosen the corset thing that went under the dress to stop it from pinching her. She refused to ask what the judge might have replied, but Eric answered her unspoken question anyway. He turned to her, his eyes were dark and mysterious in the dim light. "When I asked the judge about springing me early, he said I should talk to you."

The vise around her ribs squeezed tighter. "He did?" Why had she got involved in something that was none of her business? This was what happened when you tried to be a good person. She scrambled to think of something to say that wouldn't constitute a lie. Because she was pretty sure that Eric would be furious if he knew that she had kept him in prison after the judge was willing to free him.

"Yes, he did." There was another awkward pause. "So, I'm asking you."

She huffed out a breath. "Wouldn't you think that a man who was smart enough to be a judge could manage to keep his mouth shut about something that was meant to be confidential?"

He didn't answer.

She glanced out the window and knew she was not going to lie. Screw it, if he was furious with her for her actions, then he'd be furious.

She drew in a breath. "After you saved his life, Judge and Mrs. Bailey were willing to call your debt repaid. But they decided to discuss the issue with me first." She refused to look at him because she did not want to know how he was taking this news. "We talked it over, and, I'm sorry, Eric, but my advice was that you should continue working."

"Why?" The word was delivered in a flat tone, not aggressive exactly but not brimming with excitement, either.

"The truth is, I think it's good for you. I think, for the first time in your life, you are doing work that is hard, and you're accepting the consequences of your actions and you're taking pride in what you do. I think you spent so much of your life being the family clown and the screw-up that you don't even know how amazing you can be. There's this incredible man inside you waiting for you to grow up and I think, maybe, it's time."

He remained silent and so she continued.

"As strange as it sounds, I think that working for the Baileys is the best thing that could've happened. If you're angry, I'm sorry." She dragged in another breath. "And that is way more than I meant to say. You made me nervous and so I babbled." She cringed inwardly about the incredible-man-inside thing. She thought she'd sounded like a school guidance counselor, or his priest, and completely unlike the hot woman she wanted him to see her as.

For a moment there was silence between them. Silence so

thick she thought she needed a jackhammer to break through it. After what seemed like forever, he said, "I don't think anyone ever cared enough about me to make me clean up my own messes. The Van Hoffendams are all about image, and they would rather have their son get away with murder than be humiliated by thinking of him working some menial job." He sounded more sad than angry.

She stared at him. "You don't sound very mad."

"I'll probably be plenty mad at you around four o'clock Monday afternoon when my arms are killing me and I know my buddies are at the beach having a beer. But I also know you did the right thing for the right reasons." He pulled over in front of her place. She hadn't even realized they were close, that's how intensely she'd been focused on the conversation. "Do you really think there's an incredible man inside me?"

Okay, so maybe he wanted a guidance counselor more than he needed another hot woman in his life. At least she could give him that. "Yes. I do."

He gazed at her so intently her heart began to pound. Then he leaned towards her. "Tell me the truth, do I have a chance with you?"

Her heart was so full she simply said, "Oh, Eric," and threw her arms around him.

He kissed her and she felt that wonderful moment, that rush of excitement when she realized that she was not just someone he could talk to but a woman he genuinely cared about. Whatever happened between them, she was through with holding herself back. Maybe she was a fool and she ought to be guided by her To-Do list and her vision boards, but the truth was that while Eric might be exactly the opposite of all her sensible vision board choices, he drew her and excited her as no one ever had. She didn't feel like being sensible.

When he finally pulled away they were both breathing heavily. He asked, "Do you think I could help you carry your bags up to your apartment?"

She nodded, almost too breathless to speak. He kissed her again, one more time, swiftly, as though he didn't want to be separated from her for more than a moment, and then he let himself out of the car and sprinted around so that he was there to open her door for her. It was such an old-fashioned gesture. He reached out his hand and she put hers into it. And then he actually helped her out of the car as if she were a heroine out of a Jane Austen novel being handed down from a carriage. He flipped open the trunk and removed her case as though it weighed no more than a feather. Then he took her hand and they walked together to the door of her apartment.

He never let go of her hand, until they were inside her suite and then she didn't feel like a Jane Austen heroine anymore. The second the door closed behind them he lunged at her, or maybe it was she who lunged at him, or they lunged together. She heard her case drop to the ground and then both his arms were around her as he pulled her in close. His hands and mouth were everywhere. She felt that he was greedy for her, but he couldn't get to enough of her fast enough, and his obvious need fired her own.

She was panting, hardly able to suck in breath fast enough. His hands traced her body not in a light, teasing way that she would have expected from him, but like a starving man desperate to eat.

She kicked off her heels so she had more stability. He dealt with her sudden loss of height by simply lowering his head, never breaking contact with her mouth. His hands were at her back searching and finding the zipper and slowly pulling it down. He was so warm. Even through layers of his clothing she could feel the heat coming off his body. And she wanted it. She wanted to see it and touch it and feel it. She loosened his tie, and he shucked his coat off and let it drop to the floor. His eyes were already heavy lidded and intense in their focus.

If she didn't do something, and soon, they were going to have sex on her living room floor. And, as lust-hazed as she felt, she was fairly certain that not only was her bed going to be a lot more comfortable, but she had an unopened box of condoms in her bedside table.

But now her dress was slipping down her body. He'd dealt with that zipper so smoothly she barely even noticed the slide until the fabric brushed her legs and fell to the floor. She stepped out of it and all the rib pinching in the world was worth it as Eric's gaze focused on her body clad in the lacy corset that the bride had insisted they all wear. He put his lips to where her breasts emerged above the top and a moan of pure pleasure slipped through her lips. She took his hand, and pulled him towards the bedroom.

Once inside, she crossed the room and flipped on one of the bedside lamps so it cast a soft, romantic glow. He followed her, coming up behind her and wrapping his arms around her, running his hands down her torso, teasing her through the silk and lace.

She turned and attacked his dress shirt. He helped her, and between them they had it off in no time and one more item of clothing went sailing to the floor. Shirtless, and in nothing but a pair of dress pants, Eric was one of the nicest-looking men she had ever seen. A natural athlete, he had hardened his muscles from the physical labor and she liked the added toughness. She knew that his six-pack abs did not come from a gym workout, but from scrubbing pools, lifting rocks, digging flowerbeds and trimming the Baileys' trees.

She loved the roughness of his callused fingers and the leathery slide of his palms against her smooth skin. An impressive bulge nudged her belly and because she needed to see and know all of him, she went for his belt with shaking fingers.

Once more he helped her and the last of his gentleman's wardrobe fell to the floor. Now, nothing was between them, but a pair of Navy boxer shorts, a satin and lace corset, a pair of silk panties and thigh-high stockings.

She glanced up, and Ashley's wedding dress shone softly in the lamplight like the ghost of runaway brides past. Her hands stilled. "Are you sure about this?" He'd been engaged three months ago. To another woman.

His hands were hot as they caressed her. "Are you kidding me? I want you so badly it hurts."

She'd been confused about his feelings for weeks. Even as she tipped back her head so he could kiss his way down her throat, she said, "When did you first know?"

"When did I first know I wanted you?" Words rumbled and vibrated against the sensitive skin of her throat.

"Yes."

He paused at her collarbone. "I think it was when you stood up for me in front of the judge. I already thought you were a great-looking girl, but when you took on the judge, there was something about you. You were passionate about a cause that even my parents had given up on. It impressed the hell out of me, and I could see the way the judge looked at you with respect. And I thought, *wow*, that is a woman I want to know better."

"Such a good answer."

He pushed her gently back on the bed and began slowly unhooking the front of her corset. "How about you?"

Well, she had opened up the subject, she supposed she should give him back as much honesty as he'd given her. "I'm almost embarrassed to tell you this, but when Ashley Carnarvon climbed out the window and left me holding her abandoned wedding dress, among all the feelings of panic and horror, was a moment of pure joy that you were still free." She sighed as she accepted the truth. "I had a crush on you when we were kids. I don't think it ever went away."

He eased the sides of her corset open, revealing all of her upper body. "That's some crush."

She put an arm over her eyes. "I know. It's so embarrassing I shouldn't have told you."

To her surprise he picked up her arm and softly kissed her inner wrist. "Are you kidding? That's the best thing I've ever heard."

"Eric, I've seen the way women look at you. It must happen all the time."

"I've never wanted anyone to care about me as much as I want you to."

For the second time that evening, the only response that seemed right was, "Oh, Eric," and then she pulled him until he toppled over her and they were side-by-side on the bed. He began toying with the edge of her lacy panties and she could feel her excitement rising to the point that she knew she wouldn't have a coherent thought in her head in about two minutes. She put a hand on his wrist, "Condoms, bedside drawer."

"Cool."

But he didn't reach for one right away, instead, he slipped his hand inside her panties to where she was so very hot, and all of a sudden his hand froze. Even through her last haze she could feel something was wrong. She opened her eyes and found him staring at that wedding dress hanging on the wall. "I don't like to do this with that dress looking down at us."

Her hand flew to her mouth. "I am so sorry. I never thought. That dress must bring back such awful memories."

"No. It just feels weird having it here." He kissed her softly. "One day you will have your own wedding dress, and it won't be that one."

She gazed up at that dress, and everything it had embodied for her, and in that moment she knew he was right. It was a beautiful dress. A symbol, a fantasy of something that she thought she wanted. But what she really wanted was right here. And it wasn't a fantasy. It was a real man, with all his flaws. She was in love with Eric Van Hoffendam and whatever happened probably wouldn't follow her vision board, but she didn't care.

"Let's move it into the living room." She jumped up, and so did he, each of them wearing nothing but a skimpy piece of underwear. He took the dress down and they carried it into the living room. She laid the dress carefully over the back of her couch, knowing there was someone out there that this dress was destined for, but it wasn't her.

Once the dress was settled, he turned to her and hoisted her into his arms. She giggled as he carried her, in a style that was a little bit Tarzan and a little bit Rhett Butler, across the threshold into her bedroom. He kicked the door shut behind them, and she felt as though they were both letting go of some part of their past. He set her back down on the bed and said, "Now, where were we?"

CHAPTER 11

*E*ric was happy by nature, but on this particular Monday morning he felt on top of the world. He'd spent most of the weekend with Tasmine and if they weren't in bed, he was scheming on how to get them there. Now, he was working on the garden he'd designed and it was coming together nicely.

Something dropped to the ground beside him. He pulled the earbuds from his ears and turned to find José standing with a belligerent expression on his face. The thing he'd dropped was a chunk of green plant with a few yellow flowers. "What is that?"

"Night-blooming jasmine. It comes from Mexico. My wife grows it and I was cutting it back. It would look good here."

He glanced up at José, squinting against the sun. He'd never get an apology for the way the head gardener had treated him but this, he thought, was a kind of peace offering. He nodded, slowly, "I can find room for it."

"And move that cactus. It's too close to the lavender," José ordered.

Eric waited until he'd stomped away to let the smile out. He found a nice spot for the jasmine and planted it with care.

On his drives home he'd taken to choosing different routes, driving through neighborhoods checking out landscaping and searching out designs that worked. Sometimes he'd snap a photo.

When a property was badly landscaped, or not done at all, he felt his fingers itch to sketch a design. On one of his convoluted drives, he passed a neglected old cottage on a fairly large property with a rundown orchard and grass that had given up trying to make anything of itself long ago. A *For Sale* sign was planted out front.

He felt enthusiasm bubble up inside him, something he hadn't felt for a long time. What if? What if he bought this property and turned it around? He knew he could bring the garden back to fabulous. For a guy who'd never had to wield a hammer in his life, he was also beginning to realize that he was handy by nature. He liked figuring out how things worked and how to fix them. He suspected that he could fix up the rundown cottage. He already had a vision for how it could look.

He was beginning to realize that he'd found his passion, what he wanted to do with his life. It wasn't selling stocks or spending his life behind a desk. He wanted to be outside working with dirt and plants, making outdoor spaces both beautiful and functional. Landscape design. That's what excited him.

On impulse, he called the Realtor whose name was on the sign. When he heard the price, his enthusiasm dimmed a fair bit, but he decided to mention the place and his ideas for his future to his parents anyway. They had money. They were always telling him to do something with his life. When he got home, filthy and exhausted as usual, instead of going to his part of the house and showering, he tracked down his mom and dad. As was their usual custom on a summer evening, when his father got home from work, they were relaxing on the veranda. His mom sipped a glass of white wine and his father a scotch.

"Hey, Mom, Dad," he said as he leapt up the four shallow stone steps to join them.

His mother looked him up and down with something approaching disdain. "Goodness me, you look like one of our groundskeepers. Please go and shower and change into something respectable."

His parents never, ever referred to the fact that he worked for Judge and Mrs. Bailey. It was as though he simply disappeared for the bulk of his day and on the odd occasion when he joined them for dinner in the evening, they spoke of any other subjects but their son's disgrace. He'd been so busy with his job and so exhausted when he returned home, that he hadn't realized the extent to which they were simply in denial. He glanced down at himself. "Sorry, Mom. But I really want to talk to you both."

"We want to talk to you, too, son." His father settled himself more deeply into the expensive lounge chair. "But your mother's right. Shower and change into something decent."

For a second he wondered if they were worried that he would make a mess of their brand-new patio furniture.

"Okay. Sorry."

He ran to his own part of the house, showered in record time, and then dressed in clothes he knew his parents would approve of. Slacks and a short-sleeved shirt. He even put on socks and loafers. Now he was in the summer uniform of his father and brother.

When he got back to the veranda his parents were in pretty much exactly the same position as when he'd left them. They seemed a lot happier to see him now that he was clean and tidy. "What can I get you to drink, son?"

"Oh, just a soda. I'll probably go out again later tonight."

His parents exchanged a glance. His father went to the drinks trolley and poured him a soda with ice and lime and passed it to him.

"Thanks." He sipped the cool liquid and placed the glass on the table in front of him. He was about to launch into this project that he felt so excited about when his mother said, "We didn't see much of you this weekend." She said the words with her eyebrows partly raised in a question.

He came and went as he pleased and most of the time nothing was said about his movements. But he'd gone off Saturday morning and never returned until late Sunday night. He suspected she was gently probing to find out who he was seeing. He said, "I've been hanging out with Tasmine."

His mother's face grew sharper. "Tasmine Ford?" She said the words as if there was something unpleasant about them.

"Yes, that Tasmine." Because they knew so many women of that name.

Once more that strange exchange of glances.

"Eric, honey, I'm sure she's a very nice girl, but she's not our sort of people."

What the hell? "What do you mean she's not our kind of people? You are the one who hired her to be Ashley's bridesmaid. You seemed to like her fine when she was pretty much running the wedding."

His mother gave him a small smile as though she had won her point. "Exactly. I hired her to do a job. She's a very competent, organized young woman. But, darling, she's simply not one of us."

He felt anger begin to rise. He was an easygoing guy, but when he heard his parents talk like this he wondered if they were a couple of centuries out of date. "What do you mean, exactly? She's not rich? Because she sure as hell shares some of our DNA. She's some kind of cousin, isn't she?"

"One has a number of people who claim relationship. It doesn't make them our kind of people."

He shook his head. "Wow. I don't even know what to say."

His father spoke up. "While you were young and simply sewing your wild oats, there was a certain leeway. But, Eric, you are getting to the age where the choices you make now will affect the rest of your life. You want a wife who moves in the same social circles, who has a similar socioeconomic background, a woman who can entertain everyone from royalty to international business people. Do you really think Tasmine is that kind of woman?"

"Dad, do you really think I'm that kind of guy?" For a second he felt grateful that Ashley had been spared. She was about as good at entertaining royalty as he was, but she was a Carnarvon. Between his mother and her aunt, they'd have tried to groom her to be exactly like they were. And he'd been so close to going along with their plans to turn him into a suit.

"Soon you will be back on course to take your stockbroker's license. You know that with our contacts you'll get a good position."

He sucked in a breath and straightened his spine. "Mom, Dad, I've been thinking about this a lot lately. I don't want to be a stockbroker. I hate sitting still, I hate wearing a tie."

"Nonsense." His father stretched his legs out. "Do you think I enjoy wearing a tie? Or spending hours in traffic? Or that I like deferring to people who are half as educated as I am?" He shook his head. "Of course I don't. But we all have to do things in life that we don't particularly want to."

"But there is something I want to do. I've discovered I love gardening, and landscape design, I'm thinking of going into business for myself. I might even think about doing a degree in landscape architecture."

His parents both looked at him with similar expressions on their faces. As if they thought he might be joking. Because he was still humming with the enthusiasm that the *For Sale* sign had sparked in him, he went on. "I found a rundown cottage on a big piece of property that I think I could do something with."

"Do what?" his mother asked.

"You know, fix it up. Bring the landscaping back up to standard. I want to make something that's drought resistant, and uses natural grasses and indigenous landscaping."

"But we hire people to do that."

"Yeah. And somebody runs the business. That's what I want to do."

As his parents looked at him, speechless, he suddenly realized that it wasn't them he should be talking to about this idea. It was Tasmine. He finished his drink as quickly as he could, while the subject changed to current events, and then he stood. "Okay, I'm going out for a bit. See you both later."

"Are you in for dinner?" His mother asked.

"No. Not tonight."

In fact, he'd intended to stay for dinner. But he was getting that familiar feeling that he had on and off throughout his life that the things that mattered to him didn't matter to them. When the mood like this came over him, he was in danger of doing something really stupid. But he didn't want to act out and prove he was the irresponsible fool. He wanted to focus his energy into something useful, and productive. It simply wasn't the kind of useful and productive that the Van Hoffendams usually chose.

He changed one more time, this time into jeans and a shirt he liked and sneakers that he didn't wear to work. He threw a few things into a duffel bag, some clean working clothes for the morning, his shaving kit and a towel that wasn't purple and then he headed back out on the road. He called Tasmine and she answered right away. On impulse he said, "Do you have a minute?"

"Sure. What's up?" He could hear traffic sounds and he knew from the hollow sound of her voice that she was on her Bluetooth in her car. Excellent. He said, "I want you to meet me at an address."

"Okay. What kind of address is it?"

"It's an old abandoned cottage. It's for sale."

"Are you real estate hunting?"

"Maybe. I think so."

"Eric, do you have any idea what a cottage costs around here? Even an abandoned one?"

He groaned aloud. "Yeah. I do."

"Well, it can't hurt to look."

When she met him there a quarter of an hour later, he was already out of his car and looking at the property. The feeling of excitement bloomed again when he saw her. He rapidly pulled her in for a kiss. "I never saw you today. I missed you."

"I know. I was crazy busy. I didn't have time to come by the Baileys' place today."

"I couldn't stop thinking about the weekend."

Her cheeks grew pink. "Me neither."

He kissed her again. "I hope you have the evening free."

"The evening free for what?"

He shrugged his shoulders. "For me."

"Really? Is this how it's going to be? You just call me and give me one minute's notice and I'm supposed to drop everything for you?"

"No. I guess I didn't think about it. I just assumed you'd want to see me."

She made a sound of pure frustration. "Of course I want to see you. But I have a life. I need notice. I need some idea of where we're going and what I'm supposed to wear."

He glanced down at her high-heels and her linen skirt suit and then he glanced at the massive weeds and broken concrete that made up the garden area of the property. "I'm sorry. I wasn't thinking."

Her lips twitched. "It's okay. Luckily, I love looking at real estate."

He turned her so they were both facing the cottage. He tried to see it through her eyes, and figured it wasn't a very imposing sight. "I want to buy this place to fix it up."

"Just the garden?"

"No. The whole place."

As they stood there side-by-side he felt the moment that her enthusiasm started to bubble up. "The potential here is amazing. Can you even imagine what you could do? Does anyone live here?"

"I don't know. I don't think so."

She grabbed his hand. "Come on. Let's peek in the windows."

They ran around like little kids pressing their noses against the windows and looking inside. It was clear that no one lived there since there wasn't a stick of furniture in the house. Well, that wasn't quite true. There was a broken chair in one bedroom at the back, and an ancient kitchen table. Otherwise, it was empty. Potential was right. Potential was pretty much all it had.

"What do you think? Is it too big a project to take on?"

"Well, you said yourself you have a lot of energy. But, I don't want to be rude or anything, but where would you get the money?"

"I don't know. I've got some. But I need to get a mortgage."

"You have to have a job to get a mortgage."

"I was going to hit my folks up for loan, but they didn't seem too excited about the idea."

She laughed at that. "Did you really think they would? Eric, they're grooming you to be exactly like your older brother. Or your dad. Or Duncan Carnarvon."

"I know. But I don't want to be like that."

She grinned at him and gave him a swift kiss. "Good. Because I don't want you to be like that either."

"I'm going to call the Realtor tomorrow," he said. "There has to be a way."

"I can't imagine what it would be like to come from money."

"Honestly, the money part is good, but there's a lot of crap that goes along with it." Like the preconceived notions of what a person was supposed to be, and do, and even worse, who they were supposed to marry.

"So, can I take you out for dinner?"

"Don't you think you should be saving your money for your down payment?"

"Yes. I should. But not tonight. Tonight we celebrate."

She laughed. "And what exactly are we celebrating?"

"Today I figured out what I want to do with my life."

"Buying a rundown house is your life's ambition?"

"No. I'm going to start a landscaping company."

"Eric, that's a great idea!"

It was a relief to have someone excited about his idea. "I know. I actually love working at the Baileys now that I'm doing real gardening. I think I might even be getting José on board." He told her about the jasmine and she said that alone was worth celebrating. "There is so much potential with their property, and the cool thing is they know it." He looked down at her. "I did some research online. There's a landscape architecture program at Berkeley that I wouldn't mind taking."

She looped her arms around his neck and kissed him, she simply stared up into his face. "You know what I love?"

"What?" For some reason his heart sped up.

"I love to hear the enthusiasm in your voice. I think maybe you'd been drifting for a while, and now you have a goal, and a life plan. I love that."

"I think you are a good influence on me. I mean, you are the queen of the life plan."

"Wow, you're good for me too. You remind me to stop and have fun."

"So, speaking of fun? Where do you want to eat?"

"I've been in a suit and heels all day, and I already had one meal in a restaurant with clients. You know what I would really like?"

"No, what?"

"We pick up some take-out, or get something to barbecue, and sit on my balcony." She grinned up at him. "And we can make a plan for your business."

He closed the distance between them and kissed her. And the kiss bloomed into something as sweet and magical as he imagined this cottage could one day be. "I like that."

So they picked up some take-out on the way to her place and then sat on her balcony in the evening sunshine while they made their plan. Tasmine pulled out a note pad and began to sketch out ideas. "You have to start with the business plan. Even my bridesmaid business wouldn't have started without a business plan."

"A business plan?" He'd imagined clients, and his ultimate vision of gardens of the future, but he had never thought about a business plan.

"Yes. For instance, what equipment will you need? You may have to trade-in that fancy little sports car of yours for a truck."

"A trade in?" He loved his car.

"Absolutely. You will have to haul things like, I don't know, soil, lawnmowers, shovels and tools and trees and plants and things. You're going to need salaries, because I don't think you can do all of this yourself. Where will you get staff from? What kind of suppliers will you have? How would you get your clients? And what segment of the market are you going for?"

At least he could answer one of those questions. "I've already decided that I'm going for the really green angle on this. I think I'd like to start with larger properties because the impact will be greater and the profit will be higher. Plus, the Baileys are influential people. If they like what I do then they'll tell their friends."

"Okay." She nodded. "That makes sense. Plus, your last name will be a good calling card for other rich snobs."

Other rich snobs. He decided to let that go and assume she was teasing.

"Where are you going to get startup money?"

"The bank, I guess."

"Then you really do need a good business plan. I think you're going to probably need yearly profit projections and expenses projecting forward five years."

He really wished he'd paid more attention to the business courses at school. "You're making this sound real."

They talked for a long time, and he could see that her enthusiasm was almost as high as his.

And then it hit him. She believed in him. She believed he could create and run a business in a competitive market. Tasmine Ford might be the only person in his entire life who had ever taken him seriously.

He worked so hard for so long not to be taken seriously that it was strange to have a woman he respected helping him, believing in him, and encouraging him.

"What do you think about buying that house?"

"I think you should get ahold of the Realtor and tour the

property. Are you really ready to purchase real estate? Are you really ready to take on a renovation as well as a garden from scratch? I don't know. I think you should make a plan for that as well, and see if it works into your plan of your gardening company."

He nodded. "That makes sense." He thought for a minute, "Plus, even if I don't end up buying the house, somebody will. And they might want landscape help."

"Exactly."

They talked until long after the sun set and the sky grew dark. He reached for her hand and led her towards the bedroom. He paused beside the couch, remembering how it felt to take Ashley's wedding gown down from her bedroom wall and to bring it into the living room. "What did you do with that wedding dress?"

"Nothing yet. I can't decide what to do with it. It seems wrong to make money off it, which I could do if I took it to a really high-end resale store. But I don't know who to give it away to."

"Don't make such a big deal about it. Sell it and get some money. You know that's what Melody intended."

"But it was Ashley's dress. Ashley doesn't have any more money than I do. I feel like she should be the one to get some money for it."

"May I remind you that Ashley dumped that dress in your arms, along with the fallout from a canceled wedding, and took off?"

"I know. But let's face it, she did us both a favor."

"There is that."

He didn't really care that much about the dress, except that he didn't like it hanging around in Tasmine's apartment for some reason.

Then she rose on her tiptoes and kissed him and he forgot all about everything but the warm feel of her skin under his hands.

CHAPTER 12

asmine woke to the sounds of Eric dressing. It was dark and when her eyes opened it felt like the middle of the night. She looked over to see the silhouette of him as he dressed swiftly. "What time is it?"

He stepped slowly over to bed. "Sorry I woke you. It's five-thirty."

"Do you always get up this early?"

"I like to get to work early. It's become a habit, and now I'm used to it."

"So dedicated," she said on a yawn.

"Go back to sleep."

"I'm awake now."

She threw the covers off and got out of bed. She found some sweats and pushed herself into them, then went out to the kitchen and started coffee. "What are you going to do about your lunch?" He always had those amazing packed lunches from Millie, she didn't have enough food in the house for even one of those sandwiches.

"I'll figure something out."

She yawned. "Let me make you some breakfast."

"Honestly, don't worry about. I'll find a diner or something that's open."

"I don't want to lose out to Millie in your favorite woman department." She reached in the fridge and pulled out a few vegetables and a carton of eggs. "I'll make you an omelet."

"Babe, you don't have to."

She turned to him. He was so gorgeous even first thing in the morning with not enough sleep. "I know I don't have to. I want to."

"What can I do?"

"You can grate the cheese."

So they worked together, side-by-side, cooking omelets and drinking coffee. It was nice, cozy. They hadn't been together long but she already felt like they were a couple. It was dangerous to think that way, but she couldn't help herself. When she had imagined the perfect man for her, and she described Eric, she thought at the time that she simply had a crush on him, but now that she knew him better, she realized her vision of what she wanted had been right. Eric was exactly the man she wanted. Not because he was perfect, nobody was perfect. The great thing about Eric was that she knew that he was capable of more than he realized.

He was growing more amazing every day. Now he had an ambition and a budding business plan. She knew that she was good for him. She really hoped he would be good for her, or at least that he wouldn't break her heart.

"What are you working on today?"

"I finally got Judge and Mrs. Bailey to consider replacing the huge lawn with some drought resistant alternatives."

"Wow. What about José?"

"José has a big problem. He knows my ideas are good, so he either has to go along with them or look like a dick. And I don't think he likes looking like a dick in front of the judge. Plus, he knows things I don't, so if we start working together I think we could really do something amazing."

"Wow, I like this tough new Eric."

"Not tough. Just determined."

He ate breakfast swiftly like a man who had somewhere to be. When they were finished, he brushed his teeth, grabbed his bag, and stopped on his way out to give her a very thorough kiss goodbye.

He was halfway out the door when she said, "Hey."

"What?"

"I'll bring lunch."

"No, you don't have to do that."

"I know I don't have to," she repeated her words from earlier. "I want to."

"I'm telling you right now, if you learn how to make apple cake, Millie won't stand a chance."

She managed to kick his butt before the door shut on him and she heard him laughing on his way down the corridor.

FOR THE NEXT TWO WEEKS, she and Eric spent every moment they could together. They worked on his business plan, talked about everything under the sun and he spent nearly every night at her place.

He made her laugh, not only at the funny things he pointed out, but about herself. His teasing was gentle, but she could see that she had a tendency to over-plan and take on responsibilities she didn't have to.

She took him to a yoga class and he took her to a baseball game. And she felt herself falling deeper and deeper.

"I wish you were a closer friend of Donovan's," she said as they were yawning over coffee and she was updating her online calendar.

"Donovan? I hardly know him. Kylie's the one I know."

"Well, if it was Donovan you could be in the wedding party and sit beside me at the head table instead of down on the floor somewhere."

"Right. That's this Saturday, isn't it. I can chauffeur you at least, and think pervy thoughts when you walk up the aisle."

"Is that what you do when I walk up the aisle? Think pervy thoughts?"

"Absolutely."

"I did not need to know that."

"I'll make a note of them on Saturday and then I can describe them on Saturday night when I have you alone."

But things didn't go quite as planned.

Kylie and Donovan's wedding day started out with a shower of rain and heavy-looking clouds, but according to the weather forecast it would burn off. Of course, there were plenty of contingency plans in case of poor weather, but Tasmine hoped for the bride's sake there would be enough good weather that she could get the outdoor photos she wanted.

Eric had arranged to pick her up and drive her to the wedding. It was nice to know that he would be there. Even though by the time the wedding came along she was usually pretty friendly with the brides, with their friends she was always an outsider. But Eric wasn't. And just knowing he was there, that she could look up and catch his eye during the course of the evening made the day special for her.

They had been spending so much time together that she was disappointed he wasn't able to spend the night before the wedding at her place. His parents had some kind of dinner that he had to attend to which she clearly wasn't invited.

When he called her in the morning, she said, "Hi. I missed you last night. How was your dinner?"

"It was okay. Some friends of my parents." He didn't elaborate.

She said, "I hope the weather gets better for the wedding. Kylie was so looking forward to having her wedding pictures outside."

"Don't worry about it. According to the weather forecast the rain won't last. No offense to Kylie and wedding pictures but I wish it would really rain."

She smiled to herself. Now that he was embarking on the gardening business he took a lot of interest in the weather.

He said, "Listen, I'm sorry but I'm not going to be able to drive you today after all. My parents gave their driver the day off and they want me to drive them to the wedding."

"Oh. Okay." How strange that neither Mr. or Mrs. Van Hoffendam could be bothered to drive themselves to the wedding. That they had to turn their son into their chauffeur. "I'll see you at the wedding then."

"I'm looking forward to it. I missed you last night, too." She heard warmth in his voice and hoped they'd be able to spend some time together after today's wedding festivities were over.

She caught a cab to the resort hotel where the bridal party

were all meeting early. She wasn't a big drinker, but she'd be having champagne and wine so she opted for a cab. Two hairdressers and two makeup artists had been hired so that everybody would be picture-perfect with plenty of time to spare. She liked organized brides. They made her life so much easier. And Kylie was definitely an organized bride.

However, when she got to the suite the family had hired for the day, Kylie was not looking cool or organized. In fact, she was close to tears.

"You won't believe it," Kylie cried. For a moment all she could think of was that moment when Ashley dumped the wedding dress in her arms and she'd been left quite literally holding the bag. "Is it Donovan?"

"Donovan?" Kylie shook her head." No, it's nothing to do with Donovan, it's the hairdressers. It's a complete disaster. They canceled!"

Tasmine stared at the near hysterical bride. "They canceled? The hairdressers canceled on your wedding day?"

"Food poisoning. Can you believe it? They had a staff party last night and they all got food poisoning. Not one of them can stop puking long enough to do my hair."

Tasmine took a breath. This, in the end, was why people hired her. "Okay. This is not a disaster. I am here." She put her hands on Kylie's rigid shoulders and squeezed reassuringly. "If you or Donovan had food poisoning, that would be a disaster. This is a glitch. I will fix this." She was the first to arrive, of course, so at least she was spared the extra layer of hysteria if all the bridesmaids got into panic mode.

Kylie nodded sharply once, twice. "You're right. I'm sorry. Having hairdressers cancel is an inconvenience. It's not the end of the world."

"That's the right attitude." Thank goodness Kylie was trying to be reasonable. It gave her time to actually do something about this crisis. "I'm going to get on the phone right now and I will have hairdressers here as soon as I can."

"I know we don't even know each other very well but right now you are my best friend in the world."

It was funny how close she and her brides became. In the last few weeks before the wedding she was like their therapist, design consultant, personal assistant, and best friend all rolled into one. As much as there was always some kind of disaster, crisis or meltdown, there was also a little bit of magic with every wedding.

Because she had been involved in so many weddings, she knew all the best wedding stylists. However, it was a busy Saturday in the height of bridal season and her first half dozen phone calls got her nowhere. Luckily, the other bridesmaids began to arrive so she didn't have to make calls with Kylie pacing up and down in front of her looking closer to tears every time Tasmine received a 'No, I'm sorry we can't help you,' from yet another salon.

Finally, she excused herself and ran downstairs to consult with the hotel's special event coordinator. Who knew better how much money Kylie and Donovan's wedding was worth to the hotel? Guests and family were staying here, the ceremony and reception were being held here, and Kylie's family had ordered everything of the highest quality. Quickly she explained the problem and asked, "I wonder if your in-house hair salon could help us out?"

The special event coordinator at the hotel was a lot like Tasmine herself. Her eyes widened only the tiniest bit as she absorbed the news that they needed hairdressers on one of the busiest Saturdays of the year. Tasmine figured that along with their regular stylists they must have extra hairdressers on call. Sandra, the activities coordinator gave her a smooth, polished, most professional smile. "Let me see what I can do."

"Thank you."

She headed for the elevator and turned in time to see Sandra, in her impeccable blue hotel uniform, pull a cell phone out and hit dial even as she strode on blue pumps at top speed across the lobby floor.

Ten minutes later she received a call on her cell phone from the manager of the hair salon. Instead of sending two stylists up, she invited the bridal party to come down to the salon. Somehow, the hotel had worked magic so all the females of the wedding party could arrive at the same time and get both hair and makeup done. The two makeup artists that Kylie had hired came along and had help from two makeup artists on staff at the hotel.

Afterwards, the salon manager invited the wedding party to sit outside on the shady patio and enjoy a complimentary beverage and a salon luncheon. When they were all settled outside, all gorgeous and with plenty of time to spare, Kylie suddenly laughed. "Isn't it incredible? Because of hairdressers canceling this morning we ended up actually saving time by getting everything done at the hotel salon. I'm so much more relaxed."

"And you look absolutely beautiful."

That disaster averted, everything else went smoothly. And, at four o'clock on the dot, the bridal party assembled outside the hotel chapel.

The wedding coordinator set them walking down the aisle

in perfect sequence. She caught a glimpse of Eric as she walked up the aisle. Only years of dance and cheerleader training allowed her to keep moving when she saw that he was standing beside a young and very elegant-looking woman. Beside them were Eric's mother and father. They looked like two couples from different generations. The young woman even looked a little like Grace. Eric caught her gaze and he winked at her. She kept walking, the serene smile never wavering, but inside she was filled with confusion. Had Eric brought a date to the wedding? What the hell?

She went through the motions, the perfect bridesmaid as always. But a line kept running through her head: 'Always the bridesmaid and never the bride.' Kylie and Donovan were duly married and then the party began. Kylie's parents had insisted on a receiving line, so she was forced to greet every person at the wedding, most of whom had no idea who she was.

When the Van Hoffendams and unexplained female escort passed her, Grace said, "Why hello, Tasmine. You look lovely."

"Thank you."

Then Grace put a hand on Eric's shoulder and a hand on the elegant brunette's shoulder and said, "And I don't believe you've met Anne. She's Eric's special friend." Even the way she presented them, bracketed by her arms, made them seem like a pair.

"Family friend," Eric corrected. But she'd seen the way Anne looked at him. She did not want to be a family friend and Tasmine had a fairly good idea that she had Grace as an ally.

"It's nice to meet you."

Then Grace said, "Come along. We must let Tasmine get back to her duties." As though she was going to race back into the kitchen and cook the dinner, then run upstairs and turn down all the beds. Maybe with some help from her tiny bird and mouse friends.

CHAPTER 13

*A*fter the endless receiving line was over, Tasmine headed into the small ballroom where cocktails were served. The huge glass doors were open to the gardens and, while the rain had stopped, it wasn't sunny enough to tempt even Kylie out there.

The party was already in full swing. She accepted a glass of champagne from a passing waiter, and automatically checked to see that everything was as it should be. Bride and groom together and looking happy? Check. Best man in the vicinity, not looking like he was going to get too drunk to make a speech? Check. Parents of both bride and groom looking perfectly content? Check.

And where was the rest of the bridal party? She scanned the room for blue dresses that would indicate bridesmaids.

A male voice intruded. "Hey, if you're looking for someone. I hope it's me." It was Jake, the groomsman who had been paired with her for the walk back down the aisle. She'd already pegged him as the kind of sleazebag who thought being in the wedding party guaranteed he'd get laid even before Kylie warned her about him.

"I was looking for the bride. I'm her maid after all."

He sent her a grin so leering it made her teeth ache. "I don't think you're really a maid."

She gave a noncommittal shrug. Not slugging one of the groom's attendants was, unfortunately, one of her rules of conduct.

She walked away only to find Eric heading her way.

"Hi," he said, stopping a foot away from her. "You look great."

"Thanks. I helped choose the dresses." This was a blue, flirty number. Had she thought of Eric peeling it off her when she'd helped Kylie with her choice? Probably.

"Well, it all went off without a hitch. You must be relieved."

"I am." They stood for an awkward moment and then he said, "Anne's a family friend. My mom wanted to pick her up on the way."

"Your mom wants to pick out wedding china for the two of you."

He didn't deny the obvious. He said, "Well, that is not going to happen."

She glanced behind Eric and she could see his mother coming their way. She gave Tasmine a look so cold the temperature in the room seemed to go down a couple of degrees. She amended her expression to something much more pleasant when she reached them and Eric could see her. "Hello again, Tasmine."

"Grace. We were saying that it was a lovely ceremony."

"Yes. It was. I really see the value in adding hired brides-maids to the group. Someone with your organizational skills brings a more polished, businesslike atmosphere to the proceedings." She turned to her son. "But, Eric, we mustn't monopolize Tasmine. She's not here as a guest, remember, she's a working girl."

Did Grace realize calling someone a working girl was akin to calling them a whore? It didn't really matter. Grace had made it very clear that they were invited guests and she was hired.

Eric looked down at his mother. "Mom, Tasmine is allowed to talk to me during the wedding. And she and Kylie are friends."

She appreciated that he was trying to make her seem like one of them. But behind his shoulder yet another woman was heading their way. This was turning out to be a worse disaster for her than Ashley and Eric's wedding. The woman bearing down on them was, in fact, Ashley herself. Something must have shown on her face for Eric turned and so did Grace and they all stood frozen as Ashley came towards them looking both defiant and embarrassed.

"How has she got the nerve to show her face here?" Grace was so angered her voice vibrated.

"Mom, why don't you go and see how Dad is doing? I'll be over there in a minute."

"But I have a few things I'd like to say that young—"

"Mom," Eric interrupted. "Not the time or the place."

Grace looked at him as though he had never spoken to her that way and Tasmine had a feeling that might be true. Grace squeezed her lips together and nodded stiffly, then turned and stomped away.

Before she could say another word, Ashley stood in front of them. "Eric. I wanted to come and say hello. Hi, Tasmine."

Tasmine said, "Nice to see you, Ashley. I'll let you two catch up."

"No. Wait. I want to talk to you, too."

"I won't be going anywhere. I'm part of the wedding party."

As she walked away, she heard Ashley say, "Eric, I'm so sorry. I really want to explain."

"You don't have to." He sounded cool and fine and then there was muffled murmuring that made her think they were hugging.

She walked away, thinking there were far too many women in Eric Van Hoffendam's life.

FROM THE HEAD TABLE, Tasmine had a perfect view of the ballroom. In fact, some combination of fate and bad luck had placed the Van Hoffendams in her direct line of vision. She watched Eric and Anne catching up on old times, sitting beside his parents, who gazed on the couple fondly.

Meanwhile, at her own table, she had the dubious pleasure of being the object of Jake's leering attention. And, as he treated the free bar like he'd be giving up drinking tomorrow and this was his last night to indulge, his attempts to hit on her grew increasingly sloppy.

She was so happy when the speeches were done, and the bride and groom headed out for the first dance together. She endured one dance with the drunken Jake, and then, saying she had to visit the ladies' room, fled.

When she got to the bathroom she looked at herself in the mirror. She saw a woman who always seemed to be on the outside looking in. Maybe her dress and her makeup and her hair matched the other bridesmaids, but Grace was right. She was never going to belong with these people. She hadn't gone to the right schools, her parents didn't have the right jobs or pedigree or yachts. Eric, on the other hand, was a natural part of this world.

She was about to leave the bathroom and was wondering how quickly she could escape and go home when Ashley walked in. "Tasmine, I am so happy to see you." She gave her former bridesmaid an impulsive hug. "I should have called you before, but I didn't know what to say. I didn't plan to run you know."

"Didn't you?" She'd been thinking for a while that Ashley had shown hardly any interest in her wedding plans. Probably because she'd never intended to be there.

Ashley wrinkled her nose. "I don't know. I think I still planned to get married right up until the moment that I was wearing the dress and we were ready to go. When I thought about walking down the aisle and joining my life with Eric's forever? I thought about those poor French people walking to the guillotine. I couldn't make myself do it."

Not the most flattering thing that had ever been said about Eric, but she sort of understood what Ashley meant. "You didn't love him." Not like Tasmine did. She thought that walking down the aisle to marry Eric would be the happiest moment of her entire life. But, from the way things were going this evening, it didn't look as though that was likely to happen.

"No. I didn't." Then Ashley said, "Is everything okay with you?"

For one second she was tempted to unburden all her problems, blurt out her feelings. But the perfect bridesmaid didn't unburden or blurt. She was there to hear the problems of overwhelmed and overwrought brides, their attendees, their mothers, and any other person who needed a sympathetic ear and good organizational skills. So, she said, "I'm fine. And how are you?"

Ashley didn't need to answer the question, the answer was written all over her. There was a glow of happiness that clung to her like expensive perfume. "I didn't think I could ever be this happy."

"So, running off with the screenwriter worked out for you?"

"You have no idea. We've been traveling in Mexico, where Ben had to do some research, and then we flew to Italy so that I could meet his parents."

"You met his parents? In Italy?"

Ashley laughed. "I know. I feel like I'm living a fairy tale. You know, the kind with a happy ending."

"You *look* happy." Tasmine, on the other hand, felt like she was in a fairy tale too, only she had accidentally been given the role of ugly stepsister or some poor unnamed character who never gets what she wants in the end.

Ashley held out her left hand and Tasmine felt her eyes grow wide. "You're engaged? Again?"

"I know. It is kind of fast. But this is what we both want."

The ring was made of two different metals, platinum, maybe, and gold intertwined. Instead of a diamond she had chosen a ruby and something pale blue. It was different, unique, and quirky, exactly like Ashley herself. "Where did you get that ring?" Tasmine knew all the designers locally and she'd never seen anything like it.

"I designed it myself," Ashley said with pride. "I wanted to do something that would be different than what everybody else has. Something that means something to me and Ben. The two metals are our lives twining together. And the stones are his birthstone and mine. I've also designed our wedding rings."

"Wow. It's beautiful, and so completely you."

"Thanks." There was a tiny pause as another woman walked into the bathroom and stared at the two of them before heading for an open stall. They both moved to the outer area where a few armchairs sat in front of big mirrors with little shelves underneath that contained tissues and cotton balls. They settled in side-by-side and Tasmine said, "I need to ask you about your dress."

Ashley glanced down at herself. "This? I got it at a vintage store, isn't it cool? I think it's from the sixties." Her dress was cotton with red and white polka dots.

"It's a great dress, but I wasn't talking about that. I was talking about the Evangeline wedding gown."

An expression of pain crossed Ashley's face. "Please don't tell me I ever have to see that dress again."

"Well, that's what I wanted to talk to you about. Your mom asked me to take it away and get rid of it."

"Good!"

"But it's worth a lot of money. I was thinking that the dress is really yours, and you might like to sell it online or take it to one of your favorite vintage stores and get some money for it."

"No. Actually, make that *Hell*, no. That dress symbolizes everything that I ran away from. Seriously, I never want to see it again. Can you get rid of it for me?"

She felt so bad for the dress. It was gorgeous, and since it had been in her life she'd become clearer about some of the things she wanted.

"Yes, of course I can. I just wanted to make sure you are okay with it."

"Honestly, you'd be doing me, my mom, and my aunt and uncle a huge favor."

"Done." Now of course she was stuck trying to figure out where to take it or who to give it to. It wasn't a dress that you just chucked in a second hand store and put on consignment. It was designer original with pedigree and elegance that no one had ever worn down the aisle. She felt sad for the dress that it should be robbed of all its possibilities.

While she hadn't actually tried it on, she had definitely stood in front of her full-length mirror with the dress held up against her and imagined living the life that it promised.

"Look, I'm glad you brought up the wedding dress. I have something I want to ask you."

Oh God, she was going to ask about Eric. And Tasmine had no idea what to say. Yesterday she would have said that they were dating, probably even boyfriend and girlfriend though they had never said those words. But today? She didn't really know what she was. If this were a couple of hundred years ago she would be the mistress and the Annes of this world would be trying out for the role of young Mr. Van Hoffendam's wife. A position she could never hope to fill.

Since she didn't answer, Ashley went on. "I completely understand if you say no, but I really want to hire you to be my bridesmaid and help me plan my wedding."

She almost laughed aloud. Fortunately, she controlled herself. "You want me to be your bridesmaid, again?"

"Is it too much to ask? Here's the thing, I thought you did

such a great job. And when I talked to Mom afterwards she said you were amazing. After I left. You were the one who figured out how to handle telling people the wedding was cancelled and she said you were so good with Eric. You sat with him and helped him get through that awful day." She fiddled with the skirt of her vintage dress. "I am so sorry for what I did to him. I wish all the best for Eric but I couldn't have married him."

"I know."

"But Ben? He's the love of my life. Anyway, I feel like we weren't only bride and bridesmaid. I feel like we became friends. I'm only having one bridesmaid, and I want it to be you."

"Really? What about Whitney and Sienna?"

"First I can't choose between the two of them. If I choose either of them the other one will be upset and I don't want two bridesmaids. You are not only a good friend, but you know how to organize things. I want you there."

She couldn't go forward unless she told Ashley ... What?. She took a breath and said, "I have to tell you something. It probably doesn't mean anything, but Eric and I have been . . ." What had they been? She knew what she had been, which was falling in love with a man she believed in with all her heart. But what was she to him?

When they were together, she felt as though his feelings were as deep as hers, but they had never said the words. Even the fact that he'd shown up at this wedding with a date on his arm, without telling her, made her wonder what the future held for her and Eric. Still, she couldn't plan Ashley's wedding without telling her the truth, whatever part of the truth she could see. "Seeing each other," she ended lamely.

Ashley was suitably surprised. Her pretty eyes grew wide. "You and Eric?"

"I think he turned to me because he was upset about you. I'm probably his transition person."

Ashley suddenly leaned forward and grabbed her wrists as though about to do an intervention. "No. Don't do that."

"Don't see Eric?" She didn't realize Ashley was that possessive of her former fiancé.

"No! Don't put yourself down like that. Don't act like you're less than you really are. Believe me, I've done that all my life, and by thinking I wasn't good enough I almost ended up married to Eric so that he wouldn't have to go to jail."

"You know, he feels terrible about that."

"Yes. I know he does. But he was still going to go ahead and do it."

She couldn't argue with that. She could only hang on to her stubborn conviction that Eric was changing.

Ashley continued, "And you? You're incredible. Look at you, you have a great job with that furniture company and you have your own bridesmaid business. You're smart and you are a crazy good organizer. You are exactly the kind of woman Eric needs."

"Thanks. I appreciate the support."

"Well, since it looks to me like you're completely in love with him, it would probably be a good idea to find out if he feels the same way."

"What? Is there a sign on my back or something?"

Ashley touched her shoulder. "No. You're wearing your heart on your sleeve."

"Can everybody see it?"

"Probably only me." Then she paused for a second. "And maybe Grace."

"Is that why she treats me like I'm a cockroach that crawled out from under the couch?"

"Yeah. Pretty much. Which means she's worried. Trust me, sticking Eric with a date was Grace's idea. I bet he didn't even know Anne was coming."

"Who is she?"

"Grace has been trying to get those two together since high school. Her family's even richer than the Van Hoffendams. I think her mother's family came over with the Mayflower. Anne would probably go for it because, you know, it's Eric. But he doesn't care about her."

"Well, I've had the fun of watching Eric and Anne laughing over old times while getting hit on all night by the sleaziest groomsman ever."

"Gross. Why don't you come and sit with Ben and me? We're at a really fun table."

"Thanks. Maybe for a bit, but I think I'll head out soon."

"So, about my wedding? Will you do it?"

"I'm going to be completely honest with you. I'm going to check with Eric first. Because I do care about him. And I don't want to do anything that would upset him."

"Okay. So, if he's fine with it, will you do it?"

"Absolutely."

"That's fantastic! We're planning the smallest wedding we can get away with. We want to be married outside with no fuss." She grinned suddenly and her nose ring winked in the light. "Oh, and you know what my bridesmaid is wearing?"

"What?"

Ashley leaned closer. "Anything she wants."

She laughed. "Okay, you've got a deal. If it's okay with Eric, I'll do your wedding. When are you getting married?"

"Soon. We'll work around your schedule. We want a ceremony that is small and intimate. Us, close friends and family."

"Sounds perfect." She probably sounded wistful for Ashley reached over and said, "There's someone perfect for everyone. I never used to believe it, but now I know it's true. You'll find your perfect man."

She nodded, but the truth was she'd already found the perfect man for her.

What did she do if he didn't feel the same?

As they walked out of the bathroom together she imagined a lifetime of missing Eric, of growing old alone and talking about him to her cats.

 $\mathcal{E}$ ric had no idea why Tasmine was sitting there at the head table flirting like crazy with Jake who was an asshat, unless it was to make him crazy jealous. If that was her plan, it was working great. He tried not to spend his whole time staring up at Tasmine. He tried out of sheer politeness to hold a conversation with Anne, even though her only interests seemed to be shopping, telling him about the new property her family was planning to buy, and her upcoming trip to Paris.

He thought this was the most boring evening he'd ever spent. Plus, his mother was trying so blatantly to get him and Anne together that he wanted to run far away as fast as he could. He led Anne to the dance floor for an obligatory dance and then returned her to the table where his parents were. He excused himself and set off to find Tasmine.

He saw her at a table, laughing with Ben and Ash. He hadn't missed the glint of gold on Ashley's engagement finger. Ash had apologized to him and he'd given her a hug. The truth was she'd done them both a favor by not marrying him. A bit more notice would have been nice, though.

He wandered around the room. Toad and Slade and a few of his old buddies hunkered around the bar doing shots. Toad caught sight of him and waved him over. He could tell they were half pissed and probably headed to making fools of themselves. He walked over and joked with them a bit. Slade pushed a shot at him but he shook his head. "I'm driving."

Toad nodded, bleary eyed. "You and Anne, huh?"

"No. Not me and Anne. I gave her a lift is all."

"Sorry," Toad said, stretching out the last syllable.

When had this happened to him? When had he stopped being the fun guy? For a split second he was tempted. He could down a few shots, hang out like the old days. His parents could catch a cab.

But he didn't. When had he stopped being not only the fun guy, but the irresponsible fun guy?

He had promised to drive his parents and Anne home and now that he thought about it he suspected that his mother had given the driver the day off not by accident, but on purpose. Her heavy-handed matchmaking hadn't worked out too well the first time; he was amazed she still insisted on trying. And she was so inept. Him and Anne? Never going to happen.

When he thought about being the one at the head table, looking over at the woman he had married that very day, the only woman he could see in the seat beside him was Tasmine. He didn't know when or how it happened, but he was in love with her. And it didn't feel like he'd been put into a straitjacket the way he'd felt when he got engaged to Ashley. Being with Tasmine felt the exact opposite. Like freedom and possibilities.

He finally caught up with Tasmine as she was standing near the cloakroom with her back against the wall, and Jake, the world's most annoying man, was standing way too close to her, trying to stare down the top of her dress.

What his jealousy had prevented him from seeing earlier, was very clear to him now. She did not like Jake and she didn't want him anywhere near her. She kept edging away and the drunk groomsman kept closing the distance between them.

He walked right smack up to Tasmine and said, "Hey, sorry I got tied up, honey." He inwardly cringed at the word honey since it was a term he'd never use. He pulled her to him and kissed her lips more with ownership than passion. Letting Jake know that now would be a good time to back off.

With his arm slung around Tasmine's shoulders, he said, "Hey Jake what's happening?"

"Nothing much." He glanced from one to the other of them. "Are you two hooking up now?"

Tasmine glared at him. "No, we're not hooking up."

"We are seeing each other." Eric spoke slowly and deliberately. "And we are exclusive."

Jake put his hands up. "Hey, no problem. I didn't know." He backed off fast and Tasmine moved away so that Eric's arm dropped from her shoulders. She looked up at him, "Thanks for that. The trouble with being a hired bridesmaid is it's really not cool to kick a groomsman in the balls."

"You should've asked me. I would have done it for you."

"Thanks. So, are you having a good time?"

"Are you kidding me? My ex-fiancée is here with her new fiancé, my mother dragged me here with another woman without even telling me, and the woman I want to be with is getting hit on by another guy." He put his head to one side considering. "So, no. I would say I'm not having a very good time. But I'm really hoping the night's about to get a whole lot better."

"And is it going to get better?" He felt that she was touchy. Probably she'd been as surprised as he was to find he was here with another woman. Plus, she'd had Jake pawing her all night.

"I hope so. Can I come by your place later?" And then he remembered that he had originally planned to drive her here and take her home. "Let me amend that. Can I drive you home?"

She glanced over to where his parents and Anne were sitting talking at their table. "Don't you have to drive them home?"

He closed his eyes and let out a breath. "Yes. I do. But I'll take them home and then come back and pick you up and drive you home."

"No. That's okay. I'm tired, I'll catch a cab."

"No. Wait. I'll drive you home and then come back for them."

She shook her head. "Your mom already hates me. She'll never forgive me if I drag you away."

He took her by the shoulders. "I want to."

"I know. But what's the point? She'll only be angry with both of us."

"Can I get you a cab at least?"

She smiled. "They have doormen who can do that."

He took her hand. "Come on. I'll wait with you."

He waited while she collected her things and then dragged her case out to the lobby. Of course, cabs were lining up outside. The doorman took the bag and put it into the trunk of the cab that slid forward.

"Tasmine, I'm sorry tonight turned out this way. Can I come by later?"

She looked at him and he thought she was going to say yes. He wanted her to so badly it hurt. He loved her and he felt the urge to tell her, but not here on the street with hotel staff watching.

Then she said, "No. Not tonight."

He kissed her and got in front of the doorman so he could open the back door of the cab for her. And then he watched her drive away.

ON THE CAB ride home she wondered how an evening she'd been so looking forward to could go so wrong? She was tired of taking cabs home alone. She was tired of being the world's most efficient bridesmaid.

Ashley had told her she put herself down and she could see how that was true. She deserved better than this. Would Donovan dump Kylie so he could drive his parents and some other woman to a wedding? No he would not. Would Ben have ditched Ashley so that he could go somewhere with his parents and some single female friend? No. He would not.

Her self-pity took over the self-control she so prided herself on. Screw it, she was tired of being the perfect bridesmaid. She got the cab driver to stop at a convenience store where she ran in and hit the snack aisle. Twinkies. She needed Twinkies. And after throwing a couple of packages of the cakes into her basket, she grabbed Doritos – she couldn't decide between cool ranch and taco flavored so she got them both. And, as she hit the checkout she couldn't resist the giant bag of M&Ms.

When she got home, she removed her dress and hung it in one side of her double closet where she kept her dresses. It was like a graveyard of bridesmaid dresses. She hung them by color so when she opened that side of her closet a rainbow of chiffon and silk greeted her. She hung tonight's blue dress on one of the padded hangers, placing it between a navy sheath and a paler blue, cocktail-length chiffon. What was the point in keeping all these dresses? When was she going to wear them? They were another reminder that she was always a bridesmaid and never a bride.

Standing there in her lacy slip, she reached a decision. She grabbed as many of the dresses as she could carry and hefted them into the living room. It took her three trips. Finally, she took the Evangeline wedding gown and placed it beside the colorful heap.

Then, she dressed in pajamas, loaded The Princess Bride into her DVD player, poured a glass of wine and ripped into her junk food. She raised a glass and toasted the colorful heap of dresses. "To abandoned bridesmaids." She said. "I'll drink to that!" And then she pressed Play.

WHEN SHE WOKE up the next morning, she felt mildly hungover, mostly from the junk food. But a night of wallowing in self-pity had been sort of therapeutic. She tossed the remains of her stash before she was tempted to a breakfast of leftover Doritos. Instead, she brewed coffee and then pulled up the list she'd been making of stores that might be interested in wedding gown resales.

She showered, dressed in jeans and a blue cotton shirt, put her hair in a ponytail and loaded up the car. She headed for Melrose Avenue where three of her top picks were located. She had a list of more than ten places she could visit before choosing the right home for her gowns.

She started with her A-List. Clarice Wedding and Vintage. She didn't feel too bad about her bridesmaid dresses. With the exception of the black and white number she was supposed to wear for Ashley and Eric's wedding, they'd all had their moment of glory. But the Evangeline dress was different. She had a strong feeling that it needed to find its bride. And she didn't think she'd know the right place to set it free until she saw it.

She carried the wedding dress and one of the bridesmaid dresses into Clarice's. When she found a young helper she was told she was supposed to make an appointment. When she explained that she had some valuable outfits, she was granted five minutes with the store owner, who offered her twenty-five bucks each for the bridesmaid dresses and a hundred bucks for the Evangeline original. "Thanks," she said. "I'll think about it."

Any vintage dress-store owner who didn't value an Evangeline wedding dress was certainly not going to get her business.

She headed to the next store on her list and went through a similar process. This one was a consignment store so she would receive a percentage of the sale price. "What do you think you'll get for the wedding dress?" she asked.

The owner shrugged her shoulders. "It's a great gown. Maybe five hundred? The problem is that we're well into bridal season. You should have brought this in two months ago."

Once again, she said, "Thank you. I'll think about it."

Joe's Past and Present was her third stop.

She had heard about Joe's but never shopped there. It was a smaller store. A young and very cute guy was standing behind the sales counter , writing something. He glanced up at her. "Can I help you?"

"Are you Joe?" she guessed.

He grinned at her. "No. My mother is Joe. I'm Dylan."

When she explained her errand, he said, "You want my mom. Just a sec." He opened a door and shouted up a flight of stairs. "Mom, come down here."

Joe was a tall, lean woman with long black hair and huge dark eyes. She was probably deeply into her fifties but she had a sense of style that was timeless. She wore all black and Tasmine bet she'd been a model in her day.

Joe whistled, long and low, when she saw the logo on the garment bag. "Tell me there's a genuine Evangeline gown in there?"

"Yes. There is."

"Wow. Let's take a look at it."

When they eased the dress out of the bag, the woman moaned. To her son she said, "An Evangeline gown is like a Stradivarius violin. No two are exactly the same, but each is perfect. Who wore this dress?"

"Actually, it's never been worn. There was a . . . tragedy in the family. The wedding never took place."

"My God. This dress is a virgin."

"Exactly. I also have fifteen bridesmaid dresses."

Dylan looked at her. "Who has fifteen bridesmaids?"

She smiled grimly. "No, they're all different dresses. I've been a bridesmaid fifteen times."

He stared at her with a mixture of awe and respect. "I can't even imagine."

"I definitely want this wedding dress, and we'll take all of your bridesmaid dresses," Joe said.

"Thanks. What do you think we could get for the wedding gown?"

"The problem is that people with the kind of money for Evangeline will probably go to Evangeline. I'll put a price tag of five thousand, but I'll probably have to take three. It depends on the bride. You get forty percent of whatever we get." She shrugged elegant shoulders. "When it comes to resale any item is worth what someone will pay for it."

Well, it was more than anyone else had offered and something about this place felt right. She liked their style and thought the woman had been completely honest. "Where will you put it?" There was a small bridal section in back but she didn't think Evangeline's gown belonged with people's old wedding dresses from the fifties and sixties.

The older woman looked at her as if asking what business it was of hers?

"I'm in sales too," she explained.

The woman nodded. "No promises, but I'm thinking the store window. I have an idea for a window display with this dress and most of your bridesmaid gowns."

She nodded. "That sounds good."

When she'd given her contact information and she and Dylan had hauled all of her bridesmaid dresses into the store, she touched the Evangeline gown as though she was saying goodbye to a friend. "I hope you find your bride," she said softly. Then she walked away, feeling as though she had left something precious behind even though she wasn't sure exactly what it was.

CHAPTER 15

*E*ric called twice but she didn't pick up. She didn't feel like talking to him.

On her way home, she stocked up on groceries. Healthy food and, even though she still felt like her heart was bruised, if not cracked, she did not let herself even walk down the snack aisle. When she arrived home it was six o'clock.

She put her groceries away and walked into the bedroom to change into sweats. One positive about getting rid of all those dresses was how much room she now had in her closet.

She'd only barely finished changing her clothes when her buzzer rang, signaling that someone was downstairs. She picked up the phone, "Yes?"

"Tasmine. It's Eric."

"What do you want?" She was angry with him and not completely sure why.

"I want to come up. Can I?"

For a moment she stared blankly ahead. She wanted him to come up and yet she didn't. "Sure."

When he arrived he looked as if he didn't know what to say. "I called you. Twice. You didn't return my calls."

"No. I didn't."

"Did I do something?"

She turned her back on him and walked to the patio doors and stood looking out. "No. You didn't do anything." She'd thought about the way he'd acted while she'd watched The Princess Bride. Twice. When Princess Buttercup made demands, her young lover, Westley always replied, "As you wish." But did she make demands on Eric? No. She helped him and believed in him and loved him with all her heart. And what did he do in return? "You let your mother saddle you with a date for the wedding and didn't even tell me. You took back your offer to drive me there so you could all turn up as a cozy foursome. So, no, you didn't do anything. You didn't stand up for me, you didn't even stop Jake from thinking he could take me home along with the wedding favors, not until the very end of the night."

"I'm sorry."

She turned to him, surprised to find him apologizing.

"I should have told my mother I'd already promised you a ride. I swear to God I didn't know she'd already asked Anne to go with us, but that doesn't matter. I could have refused. I could have texted you at least so you knew what was happening." He stepped toward her. "I let you down. I'm sorry."

"Sorry's an easy word to say."

"Okay. I also told Anne that I was seeing you. And later I told my Mom and Dad that I'm serious about you."

"You did?"

"I did." She didn't ask what the response had been. She knew the Van Hoffendams.

"It's so hard to be mad at you when you apologize."

He grinned at her. "Then don't be." He walked up and put his arms around her. "You know what I figured out last night?"

"What?"

"I'm in love with you."

She searched his face and saw he was sincere. When he kissed her she kissed him back. This should be the most perfect moment, but for some reason it wasn't.

He pulled away and looked down into her face. "That's why I've been calling you all day. I needed to tell you."

She loved him so much she ached with it. He was looking at her expecting her to parrot back his words but she didn't. She said, "This means a lot to me."

He looked crestfallen. "That's it? That's all you have to say?"

"If I tell you I love you, then what happens?"

He seemed surprised by the question. "Then, I scoop you up, take you into the bedroom and make love to you until we're both exhausted."

"And if I don't tell you I love you?"

He looked at her as though this were a trick question. "The same, I guess, only it won't feel so special."

She kissed him softly and couldn't prevent herself from admitting, "Oh, Eric, what are we doing?"

"We're figuring this thing out as we go. I've never been in love before. I don't know how it works, only that everything is better when you're around. That I think about you all the time and last night, when I imagined one day sitting at a head table beside the woman I've just married, the woman I saw sitting with me was you."

He reached for her hand and held on to it. "I know I'm a screw-up and I'm not nearly good enough for you, but I'm asking for a chance."

Emotion threatened to choke her. "You really do love me."

His smile was sweet and a little sad. "I do. And one day I hope you'll love me too."

"Oh, Eric, I love you with all my heart."

"That is very good news."

Strangely, he didn't scoop her up and carry her straight to the bedroom. Instead, they held each other and talked and laughed, and she told him about her day getting rid of her bridesmaid trappings and a wedding dress that wasn't hers."

"You know what you were doing?" he asked, sounding smug.

"What?"

"You were making room for me."

Her jaw fell open. "Have you been reading that law of attraction book I lent you?"

"I couldn't sleep. It looked like it would bore me into a coma, but instead I learned a few things," he said.

He was so adorable, and if they loved each other, she knew anything was possible.

"Now that I've made room for you, what are you going to do about it?"

Finally, as he'd promised, he scooped her up and carried her into her bedroom.

ERIC WOKE the next morning invigorated. There was something about waking up beside Tasmine, who was the prettiest thing he'd ever seen first thing in the morning, that fired him with enthusiasm for the day. Even though this day was going to be mostly hauling rocks and planting the trees he'd talked the Baileys into, he was pumped.

He tried to dress quietly, but she still woke up, this woman he loved. And who, through some miracle, loved him too.

"Go back to sleep," he said when she blinked sleepily at him.

He headed into the kitchen and put on coffee but wasn't surprised when she came out a few minutes later. Without being asked she took out a carton of eggs and a huge loaf of bread.

While they drank the coffee and she started breakfast she said, "There's something I need to ask you."

"Okay."

She looked a little embarrassed, and toyed with one of the oranges she was quartering.

She was making an omelet with spinach and mushrooms and cheese and he liked to think that she had him in mind when she did her grocery shopping. Especially as she had sandwich fixings.

"It's about Ashley." She glanced up at him. "Are you guys okay?"

"Sure. I mean, it would have been nice if she'd dumped me a little sooner, but we're good. She's getting married again you know?" He shook his head. "I mean, she's getting married again for the first time."

"Right." She glanced up. "Eric, she asked me to plan their wedding and be her bridesmaid."

He stopped grating cheese to stare at her. And then he

started to laugh. Big belly laughs that made her join in. "She wants you to plan her wedding to Ben?"

"Yes. Because she knows I'm the best!"

He was still chuckling. "If I were getting married, I'd want you to organize it too."

She sent him a strange look and he felt like he'd accidentally said the wrong thing. He felt like he'd been doing that since he got here yesterday. Like he kept putting his size twelve feet into his mouth and not even realizing he was doing it.

"When is she getting married?"

"I don't know. We're working around all our schedules. It's going be really casual, though."

"Well, I hope she'll be happy. Ben seems like a good guy."

"I hope so too. And I think she will."

He passed her the cheese and picked up the mushrooms to start slicing them. "I need to talk to you about something, as well."

"What is it?"

His news lay heavy on his chest. "I told my parents about that house I want to buy. And about the business I want to start." He didn't even look up at her. He just shook his head.

"Well, they can't stop you from starting a business."

"No. They can't do that. But they do control my trust fund. That's the only way I could buy that house."

"I hate to break this to you, Eric, but most people don't get million-dollar houses when they first start out."

"My dad sat me down and he wants a commitment from me. They've been holding a job and he needs to know when I'm going to take it." He shrugged. "It's a great starting salary."

She stopped what she was doing and stared. "But you don't want to be a stockbroker."

"No. I don't. But nobody will give me a loan to start a business, either."

"Start smaller."

He looked over at her. "I know you've done everything on your own. I haven't. My family is like a corporation. They have expectations. Maybe Dad's right and having my own business is a crazy, impractical idea. He told me it's time for me to grow up."

"Well, for what it's worth, I think you've grown up a lot in the last few months. I'm on your side. Whatever you decide to do." He caught an expression of sadness in her pretty blue eyes, and he wasn't certain whether it was on his behalf or hers.

"Thanks. That means a lot."

They sat down for breakfast and by the time he'd finished all she had done was tear a piece of toast on her plate. "Not hungry?"

"I don't usually eat a big breakfast this early in the morning."

She pushed her still-full plate over to him and, because he knew he'd be working all day, he forked up her eggs.

CHAPTER 16

*J*asmine thought of herself as an optimist. She believed tomorrow would be better than today, and that if you worked hard you got ahead in life. If you saved your money, you grew wealthier. It was always better to think positive thoughts than negative ones.

But she felt a gray cloud begin to settle over her when Eric left. He was giving up. She could feel it, and declaring his love didn't seem to have changed anything. She believed that he did love her, but did he love her enough to walk away from the easy life that had been preordained for him? To step out of that comfy and richly appointed Van Hoffendam lifestyle to do work that he genuinely enjoyed?

It wasn't that she cared whether he was a stockbroker or an astronaut or if he ended up working a deli counter. But she knew that if he followed the path that had been laid out for him that Grace and Charles would do everything in their power to separate him from Tasmine. They had their eyes on Mayflower Anne. Tasmine, who'd gone to state college on student loans and sold furniture for a living, was not going to cut it as a Van Hoffendam bride. Even Ashley, who was a Carnarvon, had only been acceptable as a Get Out of Jail Free card. Now that Judge Bailey was no longer a threat, and Eric's sentence nearly completed, he was once again a great catch for some lucky rich girl.

She got through her days, doing her best to stay positive. She saw Eric nearly every day and enjoyed every minute of their time together. But always, she felt their time was running out. He had been working for the judge and Mrs. Bailey for four months now. There were only two months left and then he would be a free man. Eight weeks wasn't a very long time. Because, of course, when those eight weeks were up he wouldn't be free. He'd be in a worse jail than anything the judge had in mind for him.

Tasmine was a go-getter, and she was a wonderful organizer, but she couldn't make Eric follow his dreams unless he was willing to go after them himself. Eric was going to have to decide what he wanted.

So, she carried on. She sold her furniture, she organized weddings, and when Ashley phoned her, they found a date in the late summer that would suit everyone.

"Should I invite Eric?" Ashley asked.

"It's up to you. It's your guest list."

"I want to. He's been my friend forever. But let me know if it's weird for you."

"No, it's not weird."

"So, are you guys still an item?"

Simply the fact that Ashley had to ask that question made it clear that Eric wasn't exactly shouting his love from the rooftops. She felt like his guilty secret.

"Yes. We're seeing each other. For now."

Ashley didn't say a word and there was a beat of silence.

The furniture arrived for the Baileys' grandchildren's bedrooms and she was as excited as Mrs. Bailey was. The painters had already been in, and the wooden floors in both bedrooms had been refinished so the oak floors gleamed. Even the windows had been washed. Now, all that waited was the furniture and soft furnishings.

Naturally, she took the opportunity to eat lunch with Eric on the day the furniture arrived. She hadn't been there for a week or two and she was amazed at the difference in the landscaping.

As she was leaving, she kissed him goodbye. She asked, "Are you coming over tonight?"

"I am, but I'm going to be a little bit late."

"Oh. Why?" Usually he told her all his business.

He gave her an enigmatic look. "It's a secret project."

She laughed. "Eric, you are the least secret person I have ever known."

He seemed slightly offended by her words. "A man can change."

She threw her arms around him and gazed into the face she loved so much. "Yes. A man can change."

She went to yoga class after work and grabbed some take-out dinner but he still didn't arrive back at her place until around nine o'clock that night. He offered no explanation but there was a suppressed excitement about him. Naturally, she tried every way she could think of to get him to spill his secrets, but he remained maddeningly silent.

The next day, she received a call from Mrs. Bailey. "Would you be able to come over today, dear?"

"Of course, Mrs. Bailey. Did you find a flaw in the furniture?" She had inspected every piece before they had installed it in the rooms, and she thought everything from the carpets to the furniture to the drapes, which she had hung herself, was perfect.

"No. The rooms are wonderful. Alice's room looks like a secret garden and Joshua's looks exactly like a spaceship. But I want your opinion on another room I want to decorate."

"Wow. Yes, of course." She wondered which room it was and why Mrs. Bailey hadn't said anything before.

"Would three o'clock be good for you?"

"Yes. Certainly."

She had to rearrange her schedule, but for a client like the Baileys she was willing to make concessions.

She arrived a minute or two before three o'clock with her notebook and a case containing her measuring devices, her catalogs, and her laptop. Mrs. Bailey welcomed her with a hug, her eyes twinkling with excitement.

"What is it?" she couldn't help but ask. Mrs. Bailey appeared as excited as a young girl on her first date.

"You'll see."

She ushered Tasmine into the living room. Did she want this room redone? It was already a beautiful room, where all that amazing art dominated. The only flaw was that sad blank space in the middle. "Would you like some tea?"

"No. Thank you."

"Well, all right then. Sit down."

Tasmine sat and wondered what was going on. A few moments later, she heard the judge's voice, and the deeper rumble of Eric's. The two of them arrived in the room and Eric looked at her and raised his eyebrows in a silent question. She shook her head imperceptibly. She had no idea what was going on and clearly neither did he.

"Eric," the judge said, "we have an indoor job we would like you to do."

"Okay." Eric looked rugged and tough in his stained T-shirt and jeans that were ground with dirt and frayed on the bottom. He was in stocking feet so as not to track dirt into the house. When she glanced at the judge she could see that he looked, not excited like his wife, but sort of anxious.

"Bring in the item that you'll find next door in my study."

Once more, Eric glanced at her, and then he left the room. He returned carrying a package about the size of a painting wrapped in brown paper. "Is this what I think it is?" Eric asked. His voice wasn't quite steady.

"It is."

"Have you looked at it?" He glanced up and she could see that his anxiety wasn't for himself. He didn't want the Baileys to be disappointed.

"No. We haven't."

She sent up a silent plea that the art restorers had been able to do something. And then, as though he couldn't bear the suspense any longer, Eric ripped the paper. From where he was standing he couldn't see the front of the painting. She and the judge and Mrs. Bailey got the first look.

Mrs. Bailey put her two hands over her mouth and cried, "Oh!" And tears began to fall down cheeks. Eric fell to his knees and reached out for her hand and Tasmine jumped up to hang onto the painting.

As soon as she had it he moved to take both Mrs. Bailey's hands in his. "Mrs. Bailey, I am so, so sorry. We'll find another restorer, there has to be a way–"

She shook her head, tears streaming down her face. "Look," she said. Eric turned and saw what they had already seen. The painting was perfect. Not a hint of his stupid doodle remained.

"They said on the phone that they'd been able to lift all the pigment." The judge said. He had to clear his throat. She understood, as they all did, that this moment was about so much more than a restored painting. "But I don't think either of us believed it until now."

"They also cleaned it. It looks exactly as it did when I first saw it in the sixties."

Eric didn't say a word but he pulled the older woman into his arms for a hug. And she clung to him for a moment. Then he rose and walked towards the judge and he held out his hand and the old man rose and shook his hand solemnly. "Thank you, Judge. Thank you and Mrs. Bailey for giving me a second chance."

Her own face was wet with tears as the judge said, "Will you go do the honors and hang that painting back up where it belongs?"

Eric cleared his throat. "Yes, sir," he said quickly. When he turned to her their gazes connected. She felt such love for him, and saw his love for her in return. They had no choice but to share a quick kiss in front of the Baileys.

And then he hefted the painting and hung it back in the space where it belonged.

Mrs. Bailey said, "I think this calls for a celebration. Judge, do we still have some of that vintage champagne in the cellar?"

"We do. Eric, Tasmine? Will you join us?"

Eric looked down at himself. "I'm filthy."

"You could shower upstairs. I'm sure Ernest has something you could put on."

"I've got clean clothes in my car. Why don't I shower in the pool house?"

"Whatever you prefer."

"Tasmine?"

She nodded. "I'll stay. This was my last call of the day."

"Oh, and I do want you to do another room for us. I think our bedroom could use updating. But maybe we'll talk about that next week."

And so, they toasted the picture and the judge informed Eric that his debt was completely repaid.

Instead of jumping for joy, as she'd imagined he would, Eric had a concerned expression on his face. "But, Judge, I haven't finished the landscaping project."

"We'll figure something out."

After they'd enjoyed the glass of champagne, the judge and Mrs. Bailey invited them to stay for dinner, but Eric said, "Do you mind if we take a raincheck? There's something I need to show Tasmine."

"Of course not. Maybe you can come next week? Our children and grandchildren will be in town. I'd love you both to meet them."

"Thank you, I think we'd both like that."

They walked out hand-in-hand. "I can't believe you kissed me in front of the Baileys."

"I couldn't have stopped myself if I'd tried." He turned to her and pulled her to him for another deep, passionate kiss. "I can't tell you how relieved I am that the painting came out perfectly."

"I know. It felt like a miracle. And Mrs. Bailey was so happy!."

"You okay if we take my car?"

"Why don't we take both cars? We can meet back at my place."

"Because I have something I want to show you."

"Oh. I thought you said that so we could get out of having dinner with the Baileys."

"No. I like the Baileys. I do want to have dinner with them. But next week will be better."

She got into his car and as they headed off, she glanced over at him. "Does this mysterious expedition have anything to do with whatever you were so secretive about last night?"

"I swear, you are the nosiest woman I have ever met."

She settled beside him in his car and they drove about thirty minutes to a familiar-looking street. He drew the car up in front of the old cottage that they'd looked at when the *For Sale* sign first went up. Now there was a *Sold* sign slapped across it. She turned to stare at him, "You didn't."

"Buy it?" He shook his head. "Without my parents' help, I had no hope of getting this house. But, I did talk to the new owners. They are hiring my company to do the landscaping. They're from New Zealand and they want this house perfect and move-in ready when they get here in two months."

She was so excited she jumped up and down in her seat. "Does this mean you'll start your own business?"

He turned to her. "I already did."

"But how did you do it? You need equipment and staff. There is no way you can start a company with no money."

"I know. I had a long talk with Judge Bailey the other day." He couldn't stop the grin that spread across his face. "He took me to his own bank. And he told them that I was a fine and decent young man, and that they should give me a new business loan."

"Fine and decent? He didn't."

"Yeah. He did. And between his support and the business plan you made me, I got a loan."

"But they didn't even have the painting yet."

"I know. That's what makes it so amazing."

"Eric, I don't even know what to say. I'm so excited. And you know, with my business, we could even go into interiors as well as exteriors. My company has a line of really high-end cabinets suitable for kitchens and bathrooms. Not that I'm trying to get involved in your business or anything."

"I want you involved. Come on," he said. He took her hand and led her down the front path. "Wait," he said, and ran back to his car, returning with a sweatshirt, which he put down on the front step for her to sit on.

He settled beside her. "I see so many possibilities for this house. And there will be others. I'm going to work my ass off to make a success of this. I won't be around as much as I'd like. I need to go back to school and take some business cour-ses, and I'm seriously considering a degree in landscape archi-tecture."

And this was the slacker who'd spent most of his formative years goofing around?

"So, does this mean you're not going to be a stockbroker?"

"That's what it means. Also, I've rented a house to run my business from."

"You have been busy."

"There's one more thing."

He looked serious and a tiny bit nervous. "What is it?"

He gazed at her and she felt lost. Whatever he wanted, she knew she'd say yes. "Maybe this is too soon, but well, today feels like the beginning of a new start for me. And I want you with me every step of the way."

His eyes were shining as they stared into hers and her heart beat so hard she was sure he could hear it. He said, "will you marry me?"

She was so stunned she couldn't even speak for many seconds. Finally, she gasped, "Marry you?"

He took her hand in his. "I know it's too soon, and I'm just starting out, but there's nobody I want to start my life with more than you. And I feel like my life is just beginning. When I met you, I thought there was nothing more important in the world than cutting a joke and making guys laugh. Getting through life with the least amount of effort seemed like a good idea. And then you came along, and you demanded more of me. And when I came to you with my dreams, you believed I could do this. I don't know if I'll ever be able to live up to being the man you deserve, but I'd like to try."

For the second time that day she felt tears slide down her cheeks. "Oh, Eric. I love you so much. Of course I'll marry you. Today if you want."

He shook his head. "No. You are having a great wedding. And you know what else? We're hiring a wedding coordinator."

He dug in his jacket pocket and pulled out a jewelry box.

She'd spent the last week fearing that he was going to revert to his old life, and all the time he'd been working on a new one.

When he passed her the jewelry box, she glanced up at him. "This isn't your mother's old ring, is it?"

He chuckled and shook his head. "No offense, but I don't think my mother's quite ready to give you her ring yet." He laid a hand over hers before she could even open the box. "And this is all I could afford."

She opened the box and saw a ring that was both elegant and pretty. Three diamonds set low on a gold band.

"You can take it back and get something you like better if you want. I wanted to have a ring for you, that's all."

She thought his choice was exquisite. "I can't even tell you how much I love this."

He reached out and took the ring out of the box, and then to her complete delight, he knelt in front of her on one knee. "Tasmine Ford, will you marry me?"

"Yes, Eric Van Hoffendam. I would be honored to marry you."

He leaned over and kissed her and they sat for a while. She sighed. "When Ashley Carnarvon dumped me with her wedding dress and climbed out of the window, little did I know she was changing my life. I thought she was handing me her wedding dress, but really she was handing me her groom."

"Wait, are you saying I was a hand-me-down?"

She chuckled. "A hired bridesmaid and a re-gifted groom. Who'd have thought we'd end up together?"

"Where should we get married?"

She thought about it. "Nowhere I've ever been a brides-maid. And that's pretty much everywhere."

"What about the Baileys' estate? It's pretty much where we fell in love."

"I'm sure the Baileys don't want to host a wedding."

"Sure they do. They offered."

She turned to him, her eyes widening. "The Baileys knew you were going to propose?"

"They probably knew we were in love before we did. Mrs. Bailey helped me choose the ring."

"But, I can't believe this."

"Mrs. Bailey said I'd be a fool to let you go. And the judge said you were the best thing that ever happened to me."

"Really?"

"And you know what?"

He held her hand loosely in his, and the ring winked in the light. "What?"

"They were both right." And then he pulled her against him and kissed her.

If you enjoyed *Bridesmaid for Hire,* the next book in the series is *The Wedding Flight.* Or grab the whole series in The Almost Wives Club Boxed Set.

A Note from Nancy

Dear Reader,

Thank you for reading *The Almost Wives Club* series. I am so grateful for all the enthusiasm this series has received.

I hope you'll consider leaving a review and please tell your friends who like contemporary romance or romantic comedies.

Review on Amazon, Goodreads or BookBub.

Join my newsletter for a free prequel to my *Vampire Knitting Club* series, *Tangles and Treasons*, the exciting tale of how the gorgeous Rafe Crosyer was turned into a vampire.

I hope to see you in my private Facebook Group. It's a lot of fun. www.facebook.com/groups/NancyWarrenKnitwits

Until next time,
Happy Reading,

Nancy

The Almost Wives Club

An enchanted wedding dress is a matchmaker in this series of
romantic comedies where five runaway brides find out who the best
men really are!

The Almost Wives Club: Kate - Book 1

Second Hand Bride - Book 2

Bridesmaid for Hire - Book 3

The Wedding Flight - Book 4

If the Dress Fits - Book 5

The Almost Wives Club Box Set - Books 1-5

Take a Chance series

Meet the Chance family, a cobbled together family of eleven kids
who are all grown up and finding their ways in life and love.

Chance Encounter - Prequel

Kiss a Girl in the Rain - Book 1

Iris in Bloom - Book 2

Blueprint for a Kiss - Book 3

Every Rose - Book 4

Love to Go - Book 5

The Sheriff's Sweet Surrender - Book 6

The Daisy Game - Book 7

Take a Chance Box Set - Prequel and Books 1-3

The Vampire Knitting Club

Paranormal Cozy Mysteries. When Lucy inherits her grandmother's knitting shop in Oxford, she discovers secrets and solves murders with the help of some special undead amateur sleuths.

Tangles and Treasons - a free prequel for Nancy's newsletter subscribers

The Vampire Knitting Club - Book 1

Stitches and Witches - Book 2

Crochet and Cauldrons - Book 3

Stockings and Spells - Book 4

Purls and Potions - Book 5

Fair Isle and Fortunes - Book 6

Lace and Lies - Book 7

Bobbles and Broomsticks - Book 8

Popcorn and Poltergeists - Book 9

Garters and Gargoyles - Book 10

Diamonds and Daggers - Book 11

Herringbones and Hexes - Book 12

Ribbing and Runes - Book 13

Cat's Paws and Curses - A Holiday Whodunnit

Vampire Knitting Club Boxed Set: Books 1-3

Vampire Knitting Club Boxed Set: Books 4-6

The Vampire Book Club

A middle aged witch gets sent to Ireland to run an unusual book shop.

Crossing the Lines - Prequel

The Vampire Book Club - Book 1

Chapter and Curse - Book 2

A Spelling Mistake - Book 3

The Great Witches Baking Show

The Great Witches Baking Show - Book 1

Baker's Coven - Book 2

A Rolling Scone - Book 3

A Bundt Instrument - Book 4

Blood, Sweat and Tiers - Book 5

Crumbs and Misdemeanors - Book 6

A Cream of Passion - Book 7

Gingerdead House - A Holiday Whodunnit

The Great Witches Baking Show Boxed Set: Books 1-3

Toni Diamond Mysteries

Toni is a successful saleswoman for Lady Bianca Cosmetics in this series of humorous cozy mysteries.

Frosted Shadow - Book 1

Ultimate Concealer - Book 2

Midnight Shimmer - Book 3

A Diamond Choker For Christmas - A Holiday Whodunnit

For a complete list of books, check out Nancy's website at NancyWarrenAuthor.com

ABOUT THE AUTHOR

Nancy Warren is the USA Today Bestselling author of more than 90 novels. She's originally from Vancouver, Canada, though she tends to wander and has lived in England, Italy and California at various times. While living in Oxford she dreamed up The Vampire Knitting Club. Favorite moments include being the answer to a crossword puzzle clue in Canada's National Post newspaper, being featured on the front page of the New York Times when her book Speed Dating launched Harlequin's NASCAR series, and being nominated three times for Romance Writers of America's RITA award. She has an MA in Creative Writing from Bath Spa University. She's an avid hiker, loves chocolate and most of all, loves to hear from readers! The best way to stay in touch is to sign up for Nancy's newsletter at NancyWarrenAuthor.com or www.-facebook.com/groups/NancyWarrenKnitwits

To learn more about Nancy and her books
NancyWarrenAuthor.com